SAVAGE ISLAND

ALAN SPENCER

Listing in the Fog

Forget the global movement, forget saving the environment, and forget dying with a long list of achievements chiseled into your epitaph, Lee Branch just wanted to get his boat out of the fog. This wasn't the early morning traffic type of fog. The boat was listing through what seemed to be walls of impenetrable clouds. Add to that, it was nighttime. There was zero visibility at any angle you played it.

This was day three of their trip. They should've arrived yesterday to the secret island. The GPS coordinates had them traveling well beyond the Cayman Islands to a restricted zone. This unknown island was allegedly an illegal chemical dumping site belonging to a mix of pharmaceutical companies and big league chemical producers. Lee imagined an island hotbed of boiling concoctions. The goal of The Green Project, Lee's organization, was to investigate the wrongdoings and blow the whistle. Lee argued trees and animals couldn't hire lawyers to protect themselves. Someone had to stand up to the conglomerates and powerhouse companies who didn't give a damn about the destruction of the world.

This mission was proving to be very dangerous. Their sources gave them directions on how to avoid the border patrols and stay under-the-radar. The directions were flawless. They traveled hundreds of miles without incident. Then six hours ago, a boat had sped up beside them. A crew of seven armed individuals forced their way on board, smashed every light on their boat, and shattered the post to their wind sail. The engines were shot up by machine gun fire, and their backup fuel was stolen.

Four of Lee's most treasured assistants were gunned down brutally in those fatal moments. Each victim received four shots center masse in the chest. Lee remained alone on the boat now. He felt like he was doomed. The wind sail and the engine were useless, and Lee couldn't use the radio to send out a distress signal. Water and food supplies were dwindling, but he could make it last five days, if he exercised stringent rationing. For now, there was only barren ocean and questions repeating in his mind.

Who really provided the intelligence on the top secret island? Lee's trusted allies gave him the information. Had they betrayed him? Who were those armed individuals that shot up his crew? And why, *why*, did they not kill him too?

Lee looked on at fog and darkness. It was a lot like looking at death. Nothing to look forward to, and nothing to look back on.

How things were going, Lee would never see his daughter again. Susan Branch was thirty-five years old and a champion of the cause. She was orchestrating things on the administrative side for The Green Project, while Lee was out sailing to nowhere. Probably straight to his death, he kept thinking.

Was Susan in danger too? Of course she was, he thought. Lee prayed for her safety. What level of betrayal had been perpetrated by those he once trusted? It made him damn good and mad brooding on it. All Lee could do was squeeze his fists, and spit out curses that ricocheted off the endless ocean.

Calming down, Lee prayed for a good outcome in whispers. He got half a prayer out when he was knocked off of his feet, and he slammed into the deck. The front of the ship crunched. Water flooded into the ship. Below foot, he could hear the gargling and bending of the ship's belly giving to the pressure. The boat would sink in minutes.

Lucky for him, Lee had his backpack on. He retrieved a heavy-duty flashlight from it, and navigated his way off of the ship. The boat had crashed into a wooden dock, and the wood was solid enough to turn an otherwise healthy ship into a sinking one. Lee retreated up the dock, and charged down its length to land.

He faced a thick jungle front. This had to be the island they were investigating. By chance, or not, Lee had arrived at his destination.

Lee withdrew the .45 pistol from his backpack, and advanced into the jungle. He searched for signs of buildings, life, or any indication of those people in cloth masks with submachine guns.

What disturbed him wasn't in the distance.

It was right under his feet.

Lee dragged his flashlight beam across the perimeters of the footprint. He was standing in the middle of it. He could've walked ten paces in each cardinal direction from where he stood before touching the edge of the print. Lee observed the notches for razor sharp claws, and shuttered to imagine the creature this print belonged to.

There was something else about the print that disturbed him.

Spread out across the print was a smashed body. He couldn't identify if it was male or female, or who it had once been. Torn threads of clothing were mixed in with pulped guts and tattered flesh. The poor son-of-a-bitch had been stepped on by a giant.

He wasn't safe, that much was clear. The jungle terrain seemed to pick up on his fear. The night came alive. The .45 pistol clutched in Lee's hands became insignificant against what lurked out there.

Concussions rocked the ground. Then came the pounding steps of an enormous creature, and the shriek of a hideous bird. Thrown into the mix were the incoming steps of a stampede. Screeches and wild hissing joined in on the jungle cacophony.

The song of Lee's demise.

New sounds joined the nerve-churning choir. Tribal drumming. Bones rattled and chimed. Dozens of crude instruments played their disturbing death chords. Then the screaming from human voices, "*Yip-yip-yeeeeeeeeeeeeeeeeeei!*"

God knows what they were saying, Lee thought, as flickers of torches appeared in the distant jungle thick. Everything was coming for him at once. Lee spotted the vague outlines of humans in loincloths. Savages. They were coming for him in countless droves.

Something large swooshed overhead, and Lee imagined powerful wings batting at the air. He dove for the ground, lost his .45, and crawled on all fours to stay undetected. Cold mud was sinking through his clothes. He didn't care. This was too much to handle!

Lee howled in terror when a force smashed through a set of trees, literally uprooting them from the soil. Hundreds of stomping sounds punctuated the explosions of wood. Ravenous birds screeched in the sky, the flock now circling overhead.

He couldn't take crawling on the ground anymore. Lee retreated on foot, going anywhere that was away from this madness. He considered purging himself into the ocean, when the strange moving lights surrounded him. Dozens of sources pointed their beams at him. The blue-white lights halted him.

"Don't move!"

"Hands over your head!"

"On your knees!"

"They're sure riled up tonight."

"We're taking you in, Mr. Branch."

Wait, how do they know my name?

Before Lee could see the persons behind the lights, he took off running deeper into the jungle, and didn't look back.

Pierce Range

Pierce Range was the man sitting alone at the back of the dive bar ironically named "The Dive." The unkempt man with long graying hair and a sharp silver stubble-covered face smoked another cigarette, and finished his screwdriver. Pierce was staring out the window facing the wide-expanse of the Atlantic Ocean from the Florida shore. Pierce had been wandering the United States without a destination for eight months. His checking account dwindled down to sixty-five dollars. This bar was the end of his aimless journey; he had seen the end coming for a long time. The grizzled journeyman was ready for the climax of his existence. Death.

"I could walk right into the ocean, and keep on walking," Pierce said to his friend Skeeter. Skeeter was a skinny prick who looked just like a bug, with his bulbous eyes and a curious slit for a smile. The jerk was also a ghost in Pierce's mind. "I've reached the end of my path. I should've died when Angel and the rest of you roughnecks died in that crash."

Skeeter shook his head. "Die today? And die looking like a bum? No, Pierce. I'm not letting you go down like that. At least cut your scraggly hair, and get a decent shave first. You don't want a funeral mortician to have to give you a make-over, do you? It's bad enough that those funeral mortician guys have to shove cotton up your ass so you don't leak shit all over the place. Let's get you cleaned up before you kill yourself. Your face looks like an ashtray."

"You make some good points," Pierce said, "but I've already made my decision. What can you do to stop me, huh? You're dead."

"You have an argument there, my friend," Skeeter said. "I am dead. And you're talking to me in your head, so there's a reason I'm here, right? If you haven't gone completely psycho on me, you should hear me out, Pierce. You've got enough money for some more drinks. You might as well listen to me while you keep wetting your whistle. What else you going to do? Stare out at the ocean and cry?"

"Damn it, shut up." Pierce was getting irritated. "I'm not going to cry. It does nothing to change a damn thing, so why cry?"

"Well, maybe you should cry a little bit. Then you might realize none of this was your fault. You're taking this self-blame shit too far. I'm not seeing you die. Not like this."

"Nothing you can do to stop me, Skeeter. You're just a voice in my head. You have no power over me."

"Yeah, I'm a figment of your imagination. So think about why I'm here. Your brain is working to save you, man. It's, um, psychology, or psychosomatic projection, or whatever mind fuck nonsense those eggheads go on about. I'm your body trying to hit the self-preservation button. Why don't you just cry and mourn your losses the right way instead of hopping from bar to bar?"

The truth, Pierce wanted to cry. Really cry and purge his emotions. The love of his life had died. And the way it all happened was the ruining of him.

Pierce was a private investigator by trade. He tagged cheating husbands, searched for missing persons for families, and helped the local police whenever they needed to beef up an investigation. Angel, his late girlfriend, and her team were mercenaries for hire. Pierce was kept out of the loop on their missions. Angel would vanish for weeks at a time and come back with another mission completed, and her bank accounts fattened up with cash.

The mercenary team was hired by private companies to deal with terrorist situations, kidnappings, and other sticky endeavors that required tactical or lethal force, with an emphasis on secrecy.

It was vague to Pierce what they did, really. Pierce didn't care. That was all Angel's business. As long as she loved him, and she came back alive, what she did for a living didn't matter.

Pierce met the rest of the mercenary team, the three others being Skeeter, Shark, and Hard Case. They were all codenames they used on the battlefield. They taught Pierce how to fire various automatic weapons, and stay alive in tough survival situations. Pierce camped out with Angel and the team during various training outings and learned the ropes of being a mercenary.

A year ago, Pierce was accompanying Angel and her fellow mercenaries on a joyride in a single engine plane. During this joyride, the plane malfunctioned. They crashed. Pierce was the only one to survive. He suffered serious burns along his back and a broken arm. He was otherwise unscathed. The problem, he did his best to save Angel from the wreckage, which was the reason he suffered the extensive burns. Pierce dragged everybody's body from the flames, but they were all already dead.

Pierce quit working as a private investigator after that incident. He drove from place to place, drinking and trying to hash out his emotions. That's when he started seeing members of the mercenary team in his head. Pierce knew they were dead people, but he talked to them anyway.

He noticed Skeeter was still sitting next to him. Skeeter's bug eyes could drive him to talk even when he didn't want to say anything.

"What do you want from me?"

"I want you to live, Pierce. You treated Angel, for lack of better words, like an angel. I've never seen that girl happier. Our team, we were tight. We knew everything about each other, including our relationships. You made her very happy. Trust me."

"I loved her."

"I know you did."

"She said she could never marry me," Pierce said. This time he let the tears flow. "She kept me close, but not as close as she could've. Angel said she could die at any time. A person who served in her line of work wasn't meant to be somebody's wife.

7

Still, I tried. I thought one day when she reached a certain age, she'd hang it up, and be my wife. I guess I'll never see that day."

"At least you met someone worth falling in love with, man," Skeeter laughed, running his hand through his faux hawk. "I dated some characters in my time, and man, the bitches got ugly real fast. You'd fuck them good, then they'd unload all of their life problems on you. That's when you realized you've just stuck your wiener into trouble. Then you learn they have kids, and those rug rats are already calling you daddy, and..."

Pierce spoke over Skeeter. "What I don't get about all of this, I see you in my head, a dead man, and I see the others from the team, all dead, but not once, not once, have I seen Angel. Why can't I see her? I need to see her, I have to say goodbye."

"You think if you try to kill yourself, she'll suddenly appear? Is that it? Well, hedge your bets, my friend. Nobody made you any promises. You realize this is all in your head. I can't tell you why she's not showing herself to you. Your brain's doing the heavy lifting here. I'm just a dead guy. I left my psychology degree in hell."

"Damn you, why can't you help me? Thanks for nothing, you useless, ugly--"

"Mr. Range? Is that really you?"

Skeeter vanished.

That's when Pierce finally noticed the woman standing in front of his table. She was almost six feet tall, with long athletic legs, and the fiercest natural red hair that ran in curly tresses down to her chest. The woman was dressed like she was about to go on a safari. Also striking, the woman appeared to have been crying earlier. She was a scared child. If someone needed help in this world other than himself, it was this woman.

Pierce recognized her.

Susan Branch.

They had a history.

Susan asked, "Can I buy you a drink?"

Shark appeared, sitting at the table beside Pierce's. The Samoan mercenary hooted. "Look at the set of legs on this one! She's a walking hard-on machine. I bet she's got a TNT twat. I know I'll explode inside of her."

Shark was as bad as Skeeter, if not worse.

Pierce ignored Shark.

"Sure, I'll have a screwdriver." Pierce's voice was shaky. He hadn't spoken to another living person beyond ordering drinks, food, and hotels for a while now. "Thanks, Mrs. Branch."

"It's *Ms*. Branch. And call me Susan. We have a lot to talk about."

Shark, a whopping three hundred and twenty pounds of Samoan fury, enjoyed goading Pierce. "You guys certainly have a lot to discuss. Which hole do you jam your rod into first? You better put the blocks to this fine piece before you take that walk into the ocean."

"Fuck you." Pierce felt his heart hammering in his chest. "Leave me alone a second. I need to think. God knows what Susan wants from me."

Susan Branch was the daughter of Lee Branch. Lee was the president of The Green Project, an environmentalist group who took evasive action against those who polluted the world. They lobbied for better laws protecting the environment. Pierce was hired some three years ago to investigate the kidnapping of Susan Branch. The ransom: dismantle The Green Project, and you get your daughter back. Lee Branch wanted to both save his daughter and preserve the environmental cause.

That's when Pierce stepped in.

Pierce tracked where the kidnappers were hiding Susan, and using the training he gained from his group of mercenary friends, disarmed six kidnappers, and brought Susan home safely. The kidnappers were from a drug company dumping chemicals illegally in the backyards of a lower class sector of Missouri. The group thought threatening Susan's life would make The Green Project back off of their cause, but they were dead wrong. After meeting Lee Branch before and after the job, Pierce learned Mr. Branch wasn't the type to back off in the face of any threat, no matter what was on the line.

Susan returned with a screwdriver, and a bottle of sparkling mineral water.

"This bitch is healthy," Shark said with a growing smile. "Too healthy for my tastes. I like them dirty. I want them to teach me new tricks. This one would teach you how to knit and bake. Fuck that shit."

Susan hadn't touched her drink. She didn't want it. What was on her mind consumed her thoughts.

Pierce threw back half his drink, and decided to get to the facts.

"How did you find me? Were you looking for me?"

"No, I wasn't looking for you. Everything's by chance. It's all very hard to explain."

Susan stumbled on her words. The woman wanted to break down into tears. Pierce couldn't allow that if he was going to succeed in getting this conversation over with quickly. Whatever she wanted from him, it would be a swift no for an answer.

"Tell me what the trouble is. Go ahead. Get it out there."

Susan's face soured. Then she did burst into tears. Pierce knew he wasn't going to get anything out of this woman. He could thank the lady for the drink, walk away, take a final swim in the ocean, and end it all without turning back. Then he would finally see Angel again. *Maybe.*

One thing stopped him from putting the period at the end of his life.

Angel was sitting at the bar.

Pierce's eyes froze on her.

Angel had finally shown herself to him. Figment of his imagination or not, Pierce was so grateful to see her. Her hair was no longer buzzed as it had been when she was alive. It was long and very blonde. Angel made herself up with deep crimson lipstick and blue mascara. Angel wore a blonde wig and the same make-up when they had sex to turn Pierce on. The ruse worked with flying colors. A woman who looked like Angel could ask a man anything, and they couldn't help but agree to any terms.

Angel said this, "*Help the poor girl.*"

Angel smiled lovingly at him, and disappeared as fast as she had appeared.

Pierce dumped the rest of the screwdriver down his throat.

"Listen, I'm staying at the hotel across the street. Room 17. You're upset. Why don't you calm down, get your thoughts in order, and come talk to me then? Think about what you really want to ask me."

Susan nodded her head.

She still couldn't calm herself.

"Room 17," Pierce repeated.

Susan wiped the tears from her eyes. "Okay. Room 17. Thank you."

Pierce got up, left The Dive, walked across the street, and waited in his hotel room for the troubled woman to knock on his door.

The Rundown

Pierce sat at the table next to his hotel room's window. He looked out beyond that pane of glass, and watched for Susan to leave The Dive. So far, she hadn't made her exit. Whatever she had banging around in her head, she wasn't ready to let it out just yet. That gave Pierce time to try and understand Angel's appearance back at the bar.

How many times had he begged Angel to show herself? No matter how hard he tried, he'd only get the male mercenaries. Pierce would squeeze his hands into fists, press them against his forehead, and hold his breath to try and force her out of his head, and still, Angel wouldn't materialize.

A *GQ* pretty boy materialized with a buzz cut. He was wearing a tropical print shirt with the buttons open down half his stomach to show off his well-chiseled body. Hard Case was going to chime in, and give Pierce his two cents on the situation.

"Funny thing about women, Pierce. Even from the afterlife, women still make you do things you don't want to do. Go figure."

"Why did Susan show herself just now?"

"Well, why am I showing myself? It's your brain, dude. *You* tell *me*. You're the one who can't move on. I don't control your thoughts."

Skeeter and Shark were both sprawled out on the king size bed. They were testing the firmness of the mattress.

Shark laughed, "Hey, the springs don't squeak. You could do some real pounding on this thing. I busted my girlfriend's bed once. The bitch made me buy her a new one. Beds aren't cheap. No joke. I even had to spring for new pillows. *Unbelievable*."

"You ever do it on a waterbed?" Skeeter asked everybody. "Don't. I had back problems for weeks. It's like fucking on quicksand. The wrong parts of your body sink in, if you catch my drift."

Shark disagreed. "It's about how you contort your body. You can screw on a water bed without needing to see a chiropractor afterwards."

"If there's a pair of legs spread out for me," Hard Case argued, "I'll make it work on any bed, even if it's a bed of nails."

"Oh, tough guy," Shark said. "I bet your dick shoots bullets too. A real machine gun you've got dangling between your legs. A semi-automatic sausage!"

Pierce couldn't stand hearing their tough guy banter a second longer.

"GO AWAY, I NEED TO THINK!"

Skeeter, Shark, and Hard Case disappeared.

Pierce rushed into the bathroom. He splashed cold water into his face. Hell looked back at him in the mirror. He had seen island castaways who looked better than him.

Pierce picked up the half empty bottle of vodka on the floor. He twisted off the cap and was about to douse his mouth with liquor when Angel stepped out of the shower. She still had her long blonde hair. The strands were wet, and dripping down her naked skin. This was how he imagined her as his wife, always beautiful and smiling for him.

"*No more drinking, baby. You have things to take care of now.*"

Pierce heard knocking on his door.

Susan.

Pierce put down the vodka, dried off his face, cleared his throat, and advanced to the door. The sun was going down; it would be nighttime soon.

When he opened the door, Susan wore a subdued expression. Whatever was in her head was close to bursting out of her mouth.

"Come in. You want to sit at the table? Let's talk."

Susan closed the door behind her, and double locked it. Then she moved to the window, and closed the shades. Pierce noticed her stiff movements; she was very nervous. What happened next, Pierce didn't see coming.

He stood there without a reaction for almost a full minute. Susan began stripping out of her clothes until she was naked from top to bottom. She stood rigid in place, showing off her body as if being held at gunpoint to do so. Tears sprang into her eyes. Her chest was heaving with labored breath. Pierce processed what had happened, and finally reacted.

"No, sweetie, let's get your clothes back on."

Susan was a sobbing mess as Pierce handed her back her clothing. She retreated to the bathroom, and slammed the door closed. He could hear her weep through the door.

The poor girl, Pierce thought. He thought again to her father, Lee Branch, and The Green Project. Something dangerous had entered this woman's life, and she was helpless to fight back against it. She was willing to do anything for help, and in her emotional state, that included taking her clothes off.

Susan wouldn't be on her own, Pierce thought. He would give her the help she needed. It was the right thing to do. If Angel, figment of his imagination or not, said to help this woman, maybe it was for the best. The brain had a funny way of handling the past, and Pierce's visions of the mercenaries could've been an entire doctorate study in unusual post-traumatic stress.

After five minutes, Pierce wasn't sure if he should knock on the door and check on her. The moment he moved to do so, the door opened. Susan walked to the table fully dressed with the bottle of vodka in her hands. She was throwing back heavy swigs. The drink eventually did its job, and she calmed down enough to have a sensible conversation.

"I'm so sorry I did that," Susan said. "I've been out of my mind. I can't think straight anymore. Everywhere I go, I'm afraid someone's going to kidnap me, shoot me, or worse, chain me up somewhere, and torture me. This is the kind of people I'm dealing with, you must realize. They don't mess around. What it comes down to is I need help, and I can't get it. I don't have any money.

All of my bank accounts are frozen. So are my father's accounts. I thought if I threw myself at you, you'd pay me back by helping me.

"I'm sorry I took my clothes off. You're a respectable man, and I should've kept that in mind. I'm not thinking straight. Listen, I really need help. Everybody in our organization is in hiding. They fear for their lives, and I don't blame them. I've got a handful of associates helping me, but they're not good at this kind of thing. They're normal people; I need someone who can defend themselves and others. We're all going into this without a real idea of how to stay safe.

"Sure, I've done things out of my comfort zone for The Green Project. I've chained myself to construction equipment and bulldozers. I've thrown paint at ladies wearing animal furs. I've protested, picketed, demonstrated, and defiled property in the name of the environment, but I haven't shot a gun at someone before. I haven't had to kill someone in self-defense."

Pierce did his best to take this all in.

"What are you frightened of, Susan? Who is bothering you?"

"It's complicated. A week ago, I received a small package in the mail. It contained a disc with a short video recording on it. My dad was tied up in a chair. People wearing masks over their faces were holding machetes up to my father's neck; they said they would cut his head off and mail it to me if I didn't come to the island my father was investigating. Then my bank accounts were frozen. Fires were set at our base of operations. Volunteers and workers for The Green Project have been receiving death threats in the mail. Everybody's scared.

"In the package was a set of GPS coordinates. My father was investigating a secret island where the illegal dumping of chemicals was allegedly occurring. They're going to kill him if I don't get to that island. In the video, my father said not to contact the police or the government. If I did, they'd cut Lee's head off.

"Without my father, the organization is falling apart. I can't hold it together by myself. I've got a few volunteers from our group to accompany me to the island, but like I said, we're not soldiers. We're nothing more than paper pushers and grant writers. We need some muscle. I don't care about The Green Project. We'll shut it down. I just want my dad safe and alive.

"We're going to the island tomorrow morning. I was so lucky to happen upon you, Pierce. Talk about a chance meeting! I remember how you handled those guys who kidnapped me three years ago. You kicked their asses. You held your own; without you, I'd be dead. You saved me, and I was hoping you could save me again.

"If we can rescue my dad, I can pay you then. I'm sure we can come to some agreement."

Pierce tried to sound reassuring up against the mountain of obstacles Susan was facing. "I'm sure we can come to an understanding, yes. You're all kinds of mixed up, Susan. I'll help you. I'll go ahead and put it out there. I need something to do, or I'll kill myself."

Susan gave him a startled expression.

"Yes, I know. Don't let that scare you. Let it reassure you. I've got nothing to lose here. I'll put my life on the line. But I need to know everything about what's going on with your father and this island. How long has your father been held captive?"

"About two weeks."

"Who gave him the coordinates to the island?"

"I don't know," Susan said. "I mean, I've searched his office, his e-mails, and all of his correspondences, and everything's been erased. Somebody saw to that. They're probably the same people involved with that island. My guess, whoever's in charge of that island might've served up the fake lead so they could kidnap him, and shut The Green Project down."

"What else do you know about this island?"

"Other than it's out in the middle of the Atlantic ocean somewhere, well beyond the Virgin Islands, nothing much. My dad believed it to be an illegal dumping site. He wanted to take pictures, gather samples, and build his case."

"And you haven't called the police or anybody?"

"I've followed their instructions. I haven't contacted the authorities."

"It sounds like somebody seriously wants The Green Project terminated."

"I just want my father back," Susan insisted. "It's a very dangerous thing we're doing by going out to the island. They could kill you and me, and call it a day."

"Very true, but what choice did they give you? They're forcing you into a corner. Chances are, they want to kill you. You're right. Your dad could already be dead too."

The change in Susan's face made him regret saying that.

"Maybe not, Susan. Who can say for certain? I don't know these people, and neither do you. There's only one thing we can do, and that's investigate. If we can't save your father, we can at least take down the assholes."

"But how?"

"You let me worry about that."

Susan eyed him curiously. "I randomly pop out of nowhere, and beg you for help. Why are you doing this?"

Angel was standing in the doorway. She was dressed in her black military garb. She saluted him, then put a finger to her mouth to indicate *sssssssssh.*

Of course, he couldn't tell Susan about the dead mercenaries who told him to take the job. He had to make up something that would stick.

"If we get your father out of hot water, I'm sure he'd be willing to pay my retainer fee and then some."

"Absolutely," Susan said, appreciating his line of thinking. "Name your price, Mr. Range."

"Call me Pierce."

"Okay, Pierce. We were planning on setting out tomorrow morning at first light. Will you meet us down at the dock? You know the one, about a walk's distance from this hotel?"

"I'll be there, Susan. You should get some rest; tomorrow's going to be a big day."

"I haven't slept in days. I'm constantly thinking about what my dad is going through right now, or if he's still alive. I keep imagining the machetes those awful people were carrying in that damn video."

"You staying with anybody?"

"I have three people who volunteered to go to the island with me. We're in the same hotel room."

17

"Any of you armed?"

"Yes."

"Then keep your wits about you. I'll meet you down at the dock at first light. Hang in there, kiddo. There's one thing those bastards didn't take into account."

"What's that, Pierce?"

"*Me*."

First Light

Pierce wasn't visited by the mercenaries that night. He slept a few hours before getting up at five in the morning. Pierce showered, shaved, and slipped into a new change of clothes. After that, he walked to his Impala parked in front of his room, and popped open the trunk. He threw back the tarp covering his guns. He kept the arms stored in the back ever since Angel died. Angel enjoyed going to the target range, and blasting off rounds into paper targets. It was a classic date they enjoyed at least once a week. Better than any dinner and a movie date.

"She had the biggest balls," Skeeter said, standing beside Pierce. "Not that our group had small balls. Angel's were just so...*big*. She probably made your balls bigger by proxy. Balls the size of classroom globes. Big ass balls, man."

"Skeeter, you're a Goddamn idiot."

"I'm your idiot, pal. You're the one who keeps dialing me up in your head. You can only blame yourself."

Pierce eyed the weapons in the trunk. He wasn't stepping foot on any boat, or island, without being armed. He considered the people who kidnapped Lee Branch to be no different than terrorists. There was only one way to handle terrorists, and that was to dispatch them with extreme prejudice.

"Getting ready for action, huh?" Shark posed, studying the trunk of guns. "Now that's much better than that walk in the ocean you were talking about yesterday. I didn't want to see you go out like that. You deserve to go out like a bad ass. Drowning in the ocean is a bit too melodramatic, don't you think?"

Hard Case nudged his way between the others to get a better view of the trunk. "*Hmmmm.* I'd take the sawed off Winchester 1887, and the Mossberg 12 gauge. I like the spreader guns. If your aim fails you, then you need as wide a blast range as possible. You're not exactly a trained mercenary, Pierce. Being a private investigator doesn't make you Rambo. You're more like a mercenary with training wheels. A mini-mercenary."

Pierce chose the sawed off Winchester and the Mossberg.

Hard Case was right about one thing.

Pierce enjoyed the spreader guns too.

He was going to pack the two guns and extra ammo into a heavy duffel bag, when Skeeter stopped Pierce.

"Whoa, hold up. You're forgetting the best weapon, man."

Shark gave Skeeter a puzzled expression. "Like, what?"

Hard Case smiled mischievously. "Yeah, he's forgetting the best weapon of all. Angel got them for your birthday, remember? Two of them, actually."

Pierce couldn't believe he almost forgot them.

Two hand grenades.

"Fuckin' sweet ass," Skeeter hooted. "That'll do some damage. That'll grow some hair on your balls. Instead of killing yourself, you'll be killing some bad guys. That's the way it should be, man. You're one of the good ones, Pierce. You're your own worst enemy. Idle hands, bad memories, and booze, it's all driven you to the brink of suicide. Susan is the best thing to happen to you in a long time."

"The idiot's right," Hard Case said. "You need to get out of your head for a while. Stop thinking about dying. Exercise, fresh air, and some machine gun fire will make you feel as good as new. Killing bad guys is like yoga for mercenaries."

Pierce collected the shotguns and the grenades, and carried the duffel bag with him down three blocks to the docking port. A long line of ships lined the water's edge. He walked in front of the boats and tried to locate Susan. Pierce thought he was too early, when he heard Susan call out to him from the very end of the pier.

Pierce was greeted by Susan on a sizeable pontoon boat. Three other people were with her. The others were unloading items, and preparing for travel. Staff was an older gentlemen who was messing with the boat's GPS system mounted on the control panel. Lords was a woman Susan's age, fresh spirited in other circumstances, but terrified of what was to come in the present. Berkley was a male college professor, dressed down in jeans and a life jacket vest. He had been talking to Susan about the island right when Pierce approached them.

"What a bunch of pussy wipes," Skeeter said to Pierce. "Staff should be wearing Depends. Lords has a nice ass, but she's as scared as Susan. Staff's the kind of person who accidentally shoots themselves in the theatre of combat. And Berkley looks like a goddamn nerd who should be playing chess, or writing long equations on a chalkboard somewhere. You sure you want to carry these assholes on your back?"

Angel appeared long enough to say, "Shut the fuck up, Skeeter. Pierce can handle himself."

"I was afraid you weren't going to show up," Susan said to Pierce. "Last night was pretty weird."

Pierce said to forget about it. He wanted to talk business. "Your group armed?"

Staff paused from the GPS system mounted on the main console, and showed her hip holster with a 9mm. Lords also had a Desert Eagle pistol strapped to her hip. Berkley picked up a Rangefinder rifle with scope. Susan had a knife on her hip, and a Beretta pistol in a holster.

"Very good," Pierce said. "Then let's get on with this. Daylight's burning."

The pontoon boat's motor revved up. Staff took the reigns, guiding the boat into the ocean. Pierce watched everybody in the group, and he could sense their concern and fear. Pierce had to get the group talking. Silence increased one's fear to the point it could fester into a crippling force. This team could be done for before they traveled a single nautical mile.

Pierce asked, "Is everybody scared?"

Staff answered for everybody. "Of course we're scared. They're holding Lee hostage. He stumbled upon something big on that island, and whatever it is, they don't want anybody finding out about it. We're marching right into the lion's den. If we don't come to them, they'll come for us. We're dead here, we're dead on the island, we're dead anywhere. So yeah, buddy, we're scared. Nobody wants to die, do they?"

"I need more information," Pierce said. "Do you have any idea the extent of what's going on at the island? How big of an operation it could be?"

"Illegal chemical dumping," Lords said. "Who knows what else? It's impossible, because Lee never reported back. We've got little to go on here."

"Whatever information Lee happened upon before traveling out there, it was probably given by the enemy," Berkley said. "We were stupid to look into the matter without more information first. Lee's so half-cocked about taking down the big offenders, he'll jump into the fire without thinking twice. The Green Project has experienced death threats before, but this, this is the most dangerous situation we've ever been put in. The enemy has the drop on us. They hold every advantage. They know we're coming. We have no idea who they are, or how many people we'll be facing. Your father has put us in a very bad position, Susan."

"Nobody could've predicted this," Susan argued. "Lee was only going to study the island, see if the facts were true, and come right back. He didn't intend—"

"We know nothing about nothing," Berkley bickered. "It's because of Lee's hasty actions that we could all be dead in a matter of hours. Thanks, Lee, for putting my life on the line. Damn him."

"Calm down," Pierce insisted. "We can't turn on each other. Not now. Not when we need each other the most."

Staff agreed with Pierce. "I've known Lee a long time. He wouldn't put us in danger on purpose. This was going to happen sooner or later. These people have been targeting us for awhile now. Whatever company they are, they've had our number for quite some time."

Berkley sneered. "I still don't like it. This is all Lee's fault. Goddamn bastard."

Susan and Lords weren't sure what to say next.

Pierce had to do something to take control of the situation. Experienced or not, they were his only allies, and he couldn't have them at each other's throats.

"Stop pointing fingers. This is happening right now. People are out to kill you. Let that sink in a moment. You can't rest until these people are taken out, so no matter whose fault it is, this is our situation. Period."

"Who the fuck are you anyway?" Berkley demanded. "Why should we take orders from you? You're nothing more than a washed up private investigator. God, when Susan spotted you, you were stinking drunk, and you looked like sunbaked shit. Why listen to you? You're a nobody."

"You should listen to me, because I'm the only one even close to qualified to save Lee and your asses."

"You're a fucking joke, you vodka smelling--"

Berkley reached out to grab Pierce by the collar, when Pierce tripped him with a leg sweep, twisted his right arm behind his back, and let Berkley wail in pain for a minute.

"Calm down," Pierce growled. "I could break your arm off, and shove it up your ass. If you want out of this mission, then go ahead, jump off this boat, and swim your way back home. Whoever's fault this is, you're in the enemy's crosshairs whether you like it or not. The police can't help you. You're on your own. I'm the only one who gives a damn about your lives that doesn't have to."

Staff was begging Pierce to let Berkley go. "Please, he didn't mean anything. He's scared like the rest of us, that's all."

Pierce released Berkley's arm.

Berkley rotated his arm to make sure it wasn't broken. "Why are you with us then? You don't have to be here, and this has nothing to do with you."

"I'm here because I helped the Branch family before, and they paid well for my services. And right now, I'm a broke ass. We find Lee, I get paid."

Pierce lied about his reasons. Everybody appeared to accept his line of thinking, and that was good enough. Anything was an improvement over, 'I saw the ghost of my dead girlfriend, you see, and she told me to help you people. I was this close to walking into the ocean and drowning myself, so it's good you came along when you did. Thanks, everybody.'

Berkley didn't want to be near Pierce anymore. Everybody except for Susan walked to the other side of the pontoon boat.

Susan was apologetic. "Sorry about Berkley, he's high strung. We've been at each other's throats for a while now. We don't know what we're doing, and we're just trying to stay alive, I guess."

"Death is everywhere," Pierce said, "and it'll keep on coming. The people who have dismantled your organization are well-versed in the art of killing. Whatever secrets they're trying to keep, they'll stop at nothing to keep it hush hush. We have to play it smart from here on out, or else the next place you sleep will be in a body bag."

Susan gasped in shock, and abruptly joined her group on the other side of the boat.

"You're making friends fast," Shark said. "What a team you people make, a bunch of environmentalists with their thumbs stuck up their green asses. You're the only one who can complete this mission. The rest of these guys are useless."

"Fuck off. Not now."

Shark took the hint.

Pierce was alone with his thoughts. He stared out at the vast expanse of bright blue ocean. Somewhere out there was the secret island. It was obvious to Pierce this was a trap. The enemy brought Lee out to the island, and now, the enemy had extended their invitation to the rest of The Green Project's key members.

Shark was right about one thing, Pierce thought. He was the only one who was qualified to complete this mission.

Making Waves

The boat was six hours into its journey. Skeeter was leaning against the guardrail, studying the waters with Pierce. "So, when are you going to bang Susan?"

"I'm not going to bang her."

"You'd be entitled. You save her dad, you save her, I would say a good banging for you is in order; it's common courtesy. You save the day, you get *at least* one fuck out of it. And she has to be into it."

"I'm more worried about what's waiting for us on that island, rather than a piece of ass," Pierce snipped. "The others are right. We could be walking right into a trap. If it's a big company dumping waste illegally, I'm sure they have the numbers to easily overtake us."

"It's an advantage, but so is having only a few people. You can sneak around easier. Infiltrate their operation. As long as you don't stop to smell the roses, you guys will be fine."

"What will I do after this is over?" Pierce asked Skeeter. "I mean, I can't see myself slipping back into my old life, working as a private investigator."

"Maybe you should explore new career options. Get out there, and meet new people."

"I'll never meet another Angel."

"People lose their significant others all the time, and move on. Somehow, life goes on. Do you believe in serendipity?"

"The fuck kind of a question is that?"

Skeeter was serious. "I believe there's more than one person out there you can fall in love with at any given time. There was maybe half a dozen chicks I could've fallen in love with out there. It's timing, chance, and opportunity that allows you to pick that one person to fall in love with. What I'm trying to say is there are more women to fall in love with out there. You have to open up your mind, and not compare notes against Angel. Get me? Open your mind."

"How poetic, Skeeter. I'm sure you're full of life advice, now that you're dead."

"Or just get laid, pal. That kind of relief can move mountains."

Berkley approached Pierce. The man's gait was cautious. "Look, we got off to a bad start. This situation is just so much to take on. I teach biology to college students, and fight for the environment. I never imagined myself toting guns, and facing machete-wielding kidnappers. This is all new to me."

"Nobody imagines themselves in these situations," Pierce said. "You and your group are very brave."

"Thank you for helping us."

Berkley wasn't keen on talking much longer, so he returned to the steering wheel. Everybody else seemed cautious of Pierce, and Susan didn't like his comment about winding up in a body bag. His tact could use some re-tooling, Pierce decided.

More hours passed. Pierce wasn't sure how much longer it would be until the island was visible. The group ate sandwiches from a cooler, and conversation was at a minimal. Everybody was nervous, so Pierce kept his mouth shut. The group needed time to themselves, and he'd give it to them.

It was four in the morning when the pontoon boat's lights hit a solid wall of fog. The fog was so dense, visibility was downgraded to a matter of feet. Staff said they were forty-five minutes from arriving at the island.

Before the group could react to the fog, machine gun fire spattered from the distance. Bullets tore up the pontoon boat from four directions. Pierce could see the brief orange flashes in the near distance, but before he could dig into his duffel bag and return fire, something punched him in the back. With the force of high-speed whiplash, Pierce was thrown overboard, and crashed into the water.

Machine gunfire rattled with a dull muffled effect from being underwater. Pierce could only use one arm to paddle, and the water was so dark, he couldn't tell if he was swimming to the surface, or down deeper into the suffocating abyss.

Everything in Pierce's head was growing tighter and tighter. The need to breathe was so compelling, he imagined his skull bursting, and his lungs breaking out of his chest. Fighting the urgency for air, Pierce could overhear gunfire blasting from all directions. Abrupt and piercing screams were cut short; maybe cut dead.

Pierce wasn't sure how to fight his way back to the surface. He knew one of those bullets had hit him. The question was where was he hit, and could he stop the bleeding? Paddling his good arm was doing little to help his situation. He kicked out his legs, and kept fighting to survive.

When his face hit the surface, he swallowed up air so hard he almost choked on it. Ocean surrounded him. There was no boat or weapons being fired, or any signs of life or land.

Pierce was stranded.

What a big help he'd been to Susan, he thought. The most experienced of the team was the first to go down. He should've kept his eyes open for threats. He'd been careless.

They came out of the fog, he reasoned. Nobody would've seen them coming. Everything happened so fast, Pierce was still piecing the scene together.

Pierce struggled to stay afloat. When he used his right arm, jolts of white-hot pain threatened to sink him right down to the bottom of the ocean. Exhaustion was starting to set in as well, and he was already weak from blood loss.

Don't let yourself go, he kept thinking. *You stop swimming, you die.*

Maybe he was going to die as he intended the other night. Instead of a walk into the ocean, he'd take a deep plunge, and never be heard of again.

Pierce wasn't going to last much longer. He kept sinking down, and having to force his way back up to the surface. How many more times could he do that before he'd fall below the waterline for good?

Adrift

Pierce thought he had to be dead by now. Would he haunt some poor fool's thoughts like his mercenary friends did his own? Maybe ghosts only lived in your mind, Pierce thought. He imagined the most eccentric people, and how they probably lived like socialite kings in their own minds. They dined with royalty, slept with the sexiest people, and accomplished world-shattering feats. All in the mind, Pierce kept thinking. His friends were alive only in his mind. He was truly alone in the living world.

Something jostled his body hard, and disturbed his thoughts. He opened his eyes. Bright morning sunlight shined down on him. Pierce's mind was slow to react. He was laying against a hard wooden surface, and somehow, he ended up back on Susan's pontoon boat. The boat itself was banked against several boulder-sized rocks. The distance was obscured by fog. Even the sunlight couldn't diminish its effect, and how it blinded the horizon.

Pierce was too weak to get up. Soft breezes rifled tree branches behind him. He couldn't think clearly enough to jog his memory to what had brought him to this point.

A friendly voice called out to Pierce. "Hey, you in the boat! Are you okay down there?"

Pierce struggled to get up. He had a hole in his left shoulder. He checked his back by touching a gummy exit hole. The bullet had gone right through him, and the wound wasn't bleeding. Lucky for him, Pierce thought. He could've bled out while unconscious.

He remained disoriented while two hands picked him up, and helped him to his feet.

"Boy, oh boy, friend, you sure wrecked your ride. Looks like your boat took some bullets. You're lucky to be alive." Under his breath, "*Sort of.*"

"Where am I?"

"Relax, friend. You're not ready to carry yourself. I could tell you everything you wanted to hear, but you're barely conscious. I still see the stars twinkling in your eyes. Let me take you to safety. It's not safe for anyone out here if you're on foot. Plus, you've been bleeding. They can smell blood from miles away, and I'm not just talking about the cannibals."

"The what?"

"Never mind that. We should get moving."

Pierce was dizzy, and couldn't focus on the man helping him over the bank of jagged rocks.

"I've got a vehicle on top of the hill. I'll take you to base where we can sort you out. They'll have lots of questions for you; then you'll probably wish you were dead. What they'll do to you...*boy, oh boy.*"

Shark's voice, "Wake up, Pierce!"

Skeeter's: "You're a dead man if you let this guy help you."

Hard Case: "Take his machine gun. He's armed!"

Pierce's vision cleared up. He wasn't running on full strength until he looked up at the man helping him over the rocks. The stranger wore a dark blue painter's suit with a badge at the breast. The badge was an orange biohazard symbol. The other breast pocket had the name "Willy" embroidered on it. When the man's eyes turned to meet Pierce's stare, the left eyeball slithered out of the socket. The orb dangled three inches down by a thin strand of pink orbital tissue. The eye smacked the side of Willy's nose, then it bobbed in place. Neon green ooze burbled from Willy's open socket.

Willy dropped Pierce onto the ground, and tried to stuff his loose eyeball back into the vacant hole in his head. "Damn it, I hate it when that happens! *Fuckfuckfuck!* I just can't keep my eyes in my head these days. I've already lost half my goddamn teeth and one testicle working on this damn island. By the time I retire, what's left of me you could stuff into a plastic bag."

Words couldn't represent Pierce's shock.

His fist did the talking for him.

Surging forward like a rocket, Pierce unleashed a thundering punch that sent the strange man reeling backwards. Willy didn't know what hit him, and he tumbled down a bed of rocks like a piece of garbage. The strange man was cursing and grunting in pain all the way down to his abrupt stop near the ocean's edge.

Shark shouted, "Run, you idiot! Go man, go!"

Pierce bolted from the scene. When he had to stop to catch his breath, he was standing on the outskirts of a jungle, unsure of his next move. The air was so sticky and heavy with tropical heat; every breath he took in felt like his head was covered with a thick blanket. He had to move fast before Willy got back up and charged after him.

"Did you see his eyeball?" Skeeter was freaking out. "It just fell out of his head! And the asshole tried to put it back in. What the fuck!"

"Forget that shit," Hard Case said. "Beat your feet! Don't even try to fight this jacked up asshole!"

A staccato burst of gunfire tore up the ground around Pierce's feet. Willy, Uzi barking in tow, was charging up the hill, and this time, he didn't give a good Goddamn about his dangling eyeball.

Willy's mouth was foamy with rage. "Stay where you're at! I'll shred you with this Uzi! You have questions to answer!"

Pierce didn't have the option to run. He had his hands up to indicate surrender when the great screeching roar of a mega bird unleashed its deafening shriek. A fast moving shadow eclipsed him. Before Pierce could identify the flying creature that was most definitely not a bird, jagged talons dug into Pierce's back. He was hoisted up into the air, and flying high.

Willy was waving his Uzi in the air and cheering. "Yeah! Eat him up! That's what you get, you motherfucking tree huggin' douche bag! Go save the environment in hell!"

Pierce had a high elevation view of the island. Fog surrounded the landmass. He couldn't see anything out beyond the perimeter of the island. The boat must've idled through miles and miles of fog. This island's destiny was to be a well-kept secret. Pierce didn't feel so special being one of the few to find this hidden landmass.

It wasn't long before Pierce knew what had lifted him up into the air. He had straight A's in all of his science classes, even at the university level. He could easily identify the beast that was carrying him so far up in the sky. If the damn thing dropped him, he'd be pulverized by the fall. The elongated bird-like head was fleshed by grayish reptilian skin. The beak itself was narrow and long, and could pierce through its enemies with a powerful neck's thrust. The wings, which were a brilliant burst of bright red color, kept swooshing at the air, propelling them as fast as a single engine plane.

This can't be right.

I'm going insane.

I'm not only seeing my dead mercenary friends.

Now I'm seeing pterodactyls!

The pterodactyl had Pierce clutched in one hand, and he dangled helplessly. He could only imagine where this dinosaur beast would take him to. Maybe a nest, or a place where more pterodactyl friends could dissect him alive with their razor sharp beaks, and enjoy a nice spread of human meat.

Processing his situation was impossible. He watched the treetops of jungle come and go. He glimpsed an electric fence that stood at least thirty feet high. Beyond that barbed wire perimeter were numerous networks of buildings made of white brick, standing only two stories high. He imagined a lot of the structure rooted many levels underground. There was more to this island than scary dinosaurs and men who couldn't keep their eyeballs in their heads.

What Pierce saw for two seconds at the entrance to one of the buildings released a surge of adrenaline so potent, he dared to fight back against his predicament.

Susan was being forced into one of the buildings by a dozen of the blue outfitted goons like Willy. He could only imagine what they'd do to her, being the daughter of Lee Branch. Willy spouted his hatred for "tree huggers" only moments ago, and the Branch family was the prime example of tree hugging.

Think.

Don't die like this!

Any wrong move could drop him twenty stories to his death. Pierce would be useless if every bone in his body was broken. He did such a terrible job protecting the team when they were on that boat, he had to do something to redeem himself, and quick.

Pierce slipped into a new version of himself. He no longer feared death. He was this close to taking that final walk into the ocean only twenty-four hours ago. What the fuck did he care if some flying dinosaur wanted him for lunch? The only thing on his mind was saving Susan and her father.

The wind picked up, throwing Pierce up at an angle where his shirt and skin tore, giving him freedom from the pterodactyl's grip. He would've freefell, except he twisted his body, dug his hands into the beast's wing, and climbed onto its back. The transition occurred in a split-second, and if he ever tried it again, the feat would never work.

Pierce didn't give a fuck.

He was flying on the back of a pterodactyl!

The dinosaur was angry, throwing its head back, and shrilling like a dying vulture with a megaphone. The pterodactyl kept trying to buck him off its back.

Pierce didn't give the monster a chance. One hand slipped over the side of its head, and the other hand under its head, and Pierce cricked its neck to the side to break it. That distinct "crunch" sound awarded his efforts. The dinosaur's body went limp.

Oh no.

Oh shit!

He was headed straight down at increasing speeds.

They were going to crash.

Crash Landing

Pierce dug his fingers into the pterodactyl's back. Speeding down faster and faster, Pierce closed his eyes against the wind smacking him in the face. He heard the smash of the dinosaur's body connect into several trees. Twisting and turning, changing directions five times before landing upside down in a tree, the dinosaur's body was perched haphazardly between three tree branches. One slight movement, and its body could fall between the limbs. Pierce was stealthy dismounting the beast and latching onto the tree. Carefully dismounting the tropical looking tree, he managed to touch his feet on the ground safely.

He was standing in the thick of jungle. One direction was identical to any other. Where had he seen that building beyond the electric fences? Pierce had no compass. He couldn't see the sun from his vantage point either.

"You have to find the sun," Skeeter advised. "Maybe it'll lead you back to the ocean. You need to get off this island, somehow. You can build a raft out of raw materials."

"He's not going to run away," Shark said, standing at the other side of Pierce. "This boy's ready to kick some ass. He's not leaving Susan behind without tagging that sweet ass first."

Hard Case was sitting on a half-rotted log. "All of you are forgetting about that flying dinosaur. You can't fist fight with a dinosaur. Pierce will lose."

Shark threw a broken stick at Hard Case. "You kidding me? He snapped that dinosaur's neck! Pure badass. Pierce has got this situation under control. Dial him up, he'll get the job done."

Pierce squeezed his eyes shut tight. This wasn't the best time to see and hear the ghosts of his mind argue like a bunch of angry apes. He was drenched in sweat. If he didn't get water soon, he would become dehydrated.

Pierce whipped around when he heard the crunch of leaves. A bated breath turned into angry words. "It's you. *Unbelievable*."

A strange buzzing sound was coming closer and closer. It sounded like a tin can stuffed with roaring flies. The noises were closing in, and fast. Pierce could see them from afar. They were mosquitoes the size of softballs. Each had blue-green bulbous eyes, and a proboscis as long as a steak knife. The bugs were streaks of motion.

"Get down," Berkley said in a hushed voice. "There must be a carcass nearby. Come on, hot shot. Down on the ground, *now*. Let's pray they don't smell us."

They hit the ground, and barely avoided the mosquitoes. They roared through the jungle, searching for the next freshly dead thing to devour. Pierce imagined how hard those dagger proboscis tubes could suck the blood out of an organism, and he did not want to be that organism.

Berkley got up from the ground, as did Pierce. Berkley was drenched, as if he'd jumped into a body of water recently. The side of his head was covered in blood from a small gash across his forehead. The old man's eyes were buggy and incensed. Berkley carried a 9mm in one hand, and a sharp stick in the other. Pierce imagined the stick as something that could be driven through a vampire's heart, and then some.

"You were the first to go down when the shit started," Berkley said, accusingly. "Susan said you were the expert. That you knew what you were doing. And *you're* the first to go down. Susan believed in you. She acted like you were going to save the day. You're no better than the rest of us. You're no better than a washed up has been.

"I don't need you, you big shot, tough guy, machismo, asshole. I got away from those henchmen by myself. I can handle this without your help. I'm not going to let those awful, hideous people ever touch me again. This island's a cesspool of chemicals and…and…and I saw a pack of raptors. Like ten of them! It'd be amazing, if I wasn't risking my life to see it.

"We're going to save Susan and Lee, and blow the lid off this island. We'll show them what environmentalists can do when they put their minds to it. We don't need money, or power, or corporate bullshit to get results. We'll show them! And we don't need no mercenary wannabe's help. You might as well turn around, and forget you ever met us. Your services are no longer required."

Pierce wanted to tell Berkley to take a pill. That they were in this together. Nobody was equipped to take on this situation, be it a man of nature, or a man of war. Berkley must've been whapped upside the head too hard by whatever had caused his dumb dome to bleed, Pierce reasoned. Still, Pierce had to choose his words wisely. Diplomacy was the name of the—

Whomp.

A wooden staff pierced through Berkley's chest with such force, he was thrown up against a tree and impaled. The sound of breaking sternum bones punctuated the damage. Berkley's body went limp. The man's eyes didn't close in death. They looked on in fearful reverence.

Pierce had no chance to compute Berkley's death.

Hundreds of wild calls followed the moment of violence: "*Yip-yip-yip-yip-yiggggggggh!*"

They arrived from every direction, and were rushing in at Pierce. Arrows, spears, blow darts, and wooden staffs were sailing towards Pierce. Pierce leapt forward, and lunged into the woods, frantic to escape certain death yet again!

Pierce only got a brief glimpse of the angry mob of jungle people. They were naked except for the tatters of loincloths covering their genitals. Men and women alike were decorated in brownish-red war paint—what could've been the dried blood of an animal or a human.

What was more concerning, their skin was covered in bubbling sores. Pus and yellow fluids leaked from those sores. Whoever these native tribal people were, they had suffered strange mutations. Some had extra arms and legs, and a few had an extra head or two! A few had hearts and intestines that were on the outside of their bodies, and covered in a clear filmy substance. He imagined the film to be a cross between gel and snot.

The ground dropped beneath his feet before Pierce could make sense of the mutations. He tumbled down a hill, and landed in a pit of picked clean human bones. He was wading in hundreds and hundreds of broken up human skeletons. Up over the edge of the pit, what looked more like a bowl, the indigenous people were waving spears and crude wooden weapons. They were coming in after him to do cannibal things.

Pierce was helpless to stop them.

The cannibals would feast.

Time to Eat

Forced out of the pit of human skeletal remains by the raving mad cannibals, Pierce was pulled in every direction. The tribes were chanting, cheering, raving, and screeching nonsense. Pierce jerked his arms, and tried to rip free from their holds. If he managed to shake off one grip, a new set of hands would quickly reclaim him. His hair was being yanked and nearly torn from the roots. These awful maniacs wanted to savage him.

New evidence of their intentions soon appeared after they hiked through half a mile of dense jungle foliage. These strange people were using crude stone hatchets, sharpened bones (both human and dinosaur) to clear the jungle thick. Huddles of straw huts appeared in a circular clearing up ahead. Dead center of that clearing was a stage for brutality.

A great pit of fire featured a spit where two sets of human ribs were sizzling and cooking. The meat smell was horrible to take in. One, because Pierce was weakened by hunger, and two, because he saw Staff's head hanging from a rope nearby. The rest of Staff's body was picked clean of meat except for his feet, which dangled from the skeleton body, dripping blood. Huddles of tribe people who hadn't hunted Pierce down were noshing down on human innards, and chewing them with the fervor of someone freshly reintroduced to the pleasures of eating. Gristle and fat were flensed from bone, and devoured with smiles painted on by blood.

A circle of children were fighting over a spleen, and laughing like children should while playing childish games. Stone hatchets were chopping up pink and purple cutlets of half-cooked flesh as the group continued their carnal feast.

Savages.

Murdering bastards.

Bloodthirsty cannibals.

Pierce renewed his efforts to escape their clutches. He stopped when he heard the piercing screams of a woman.

Lords was strapped down to a table created by laying down three trees stripped of their bark. She was naked and writhing under the restraints of several bands of rope. Lords's eyes met Pierce's for a split second. She called out the first part of his name right when a cannibal woman smashed a large rock over her head to end her screams.

Dozens of stone hatchet-wielding savages rendered her body into thirty pieces in under thirty seconds. Hunks of flesh and spatters of blood covered the band of cannibals. One held a long tongue freshly ripped from Lords' mouth, and played his own tongue along the piece of meat before chewing it with extreme voraciousness. Hands, feet, legs, and intestines were all dumped into a steel cauldron, and cooked over a bed of red-hot coals. One of the cannibals had strayed from the group to play with two bloody breasts. The sick savage kept squeezing and squeezing them. Two women were fighting over Lords' scalped head of hair.

Pierce couldn't take anymore.

The truth was setting in.

He was next on the menu.

Shark was standing among the cannibals. His face was a mask of shock. "You got to do something, dude. They'll eat you from head to toe. They're giving you the hungry eyes. I'm feeling uncomfortable, and I'm dead."

Skeeter's frightened expression mirrored Shark's. "Whoa, man. I'm sorry, Pierce. You don't deserve this. You should've taken that walk in the ocean while you had the chance."

"No, fuck that noise," Hard Case raged. "The only way to beat an enemy like this is to outdo them. Show them up. Come on! You're not dying like this. Not now, not today, never! Angel would want you to fight. Fucking bring it! Break some skulls!"

That got Pierce fuming mad.

These cannibals weren't going to eat a single nugget of flesh from his body.

The tribe was about to turn on him. One adorned in a headdress made of human bones, various sticks and twigs, and numerous dried out snakeskins approached Pierce. This could've been the chief. Pierce didn't understand cannibal tribe politics, nor did he give a good Goddamn. The chief's leathery, calloused hands played over his chest and biceps. Then the hand touched his chin lovingly. Pierce imagined a butcher ogling the fattest pig in the pen, and the son-of-a-bitch getting a stomach erection.

"Show them what brutality really means," Hard Case roared. "Now's your chance!"

Pierce didn't think.

He acted on sheer impulse.

"*Raaaaaaaaaaaaaaaaaaaaaaaaaah!*"

Pierce bit down on the chief's nose, clamped down his teeth, and bit through cartilage and flesh. He spat out the nose. The chief's exposed sinuses were burbling up blood. The chief was howling in terror. He fell backwards, and his face kept spewing blood.

This time Pierce threw aside his captors. He hit the ground, rolled forward, and stole a stone hatchet. He ran to the fire, and managed to steal a long stick that was burning at the end. Pierce clutched both, ready to kill anybody who dared to come close enough to suffer the business end of blunt force and fire.

The cannibals ran screaming in the other direction.

"Yeah, that's right. Fuck you! The meat market's closet. Get your meat off some other poor son-of-a-bitch's back!"

Pierce stopped.

He realized his mistake.

The cannibals weren't afraid of him.

A greater threat loomed near.

Run For Your Life

This was something out of a fucking textbook. Pierce strained his neck to look up so high, and take in its entire body. Every step it took, it rocked the earth. The great beast threw back its head, and unleashed a monstrous cry. The cannibals scattered. They were smart, Pierce realized, as he watched the cannibals race to a hole previously dug up in the ground. The group had disappeared underground in less than ten seconds. At the front of the hole, a door of bamboo covered in long wooden spears carved to sharp perfection threatened to cut any menace that dared to try and bash through the barrier. That left Pierce standing there with a stone axe, and a torch slowly trying to go out.

The weapons would do very little against the T-Rex.

This time, the mercenaries in his head didn't show up to give him courage.

Pierce was on his own.

Another screech left its angry mouth before the T-Rex stomped after Pierce. Pierce threw aside the weapons, and ran like hell.

Doom. Doom. Doom. Doom.

The stomping sounded just like his future.

Doom.

Doom.

Doom.

The reptilian tail bashed the sides of trees. The T-Rex's body itself was battering aside trees, snapping them like nothing but twigs. A fifty-foot long shard of tree spun over Pierce's head before bouncing twice, and rolling down a hill.

Goddamn, that was close!

Pierce got a brief glimpse of the island in the far distance.

From another pocket of the island, dozens of velociraptors, stegosauruses, and brontosauruses were fleeing from ten speeding jeeps. A large machine gun was pumping hundreds of rounds a minute at the fleeing reptiles from each vehicle. The men in the dark blue painter's suits were laughing it up as they watched the dinosaurs run for their lives. Behind those jeeps, a large semi-truck carried a bed of biohazard barrels across the crudely built road.

Pierce lost sight of them.

The T-Rex had little trouble catching up to him. The giant was at his heels. This was it, Pierce thought. He avoided being disembodied and devoured by cannibals, only to be swallowed whole by a ravenous dinosaur.

Pierce couldn't feel his body anymore. He was outside of himself, driven out of his body by fear. Still running, still hoping there was a way to survive this insane encounter, Pierce experienced a new burst of energy. He raced to the beacon up ahead knowing, he was thrusting himself from one dangerous option to another. One option had zero possibility of survival, while the other had a thin sliver of a happy ending.

Fuck it.

I have nothing to lose.

Pierce cut through the jungle, and reached the end of a cliff. Near the edge was a waterfall that dropped he didn't know how many stories, to a great pool of clear blue water.

Racing to the edge of the cliff, Pierce jumped for his life, and prayed the T-Rex didn't take the plunge with him.

Over The Falls

The drop wasn't like in the movies where time slows down for dramatic impact. In under five seconds, Pierce went from being airborne to plunging down into a deep body of water. He was already weakened from sprinting from the T-Rex, and had little strength to lift himself back to the surface. Somehow, he managed to fight his way back to air, and stay afloat. Deciding it was best to stay out of the open, he paddled towards the waterfall itself. He could take shelter behind the falling threads of water. Pierce crawled up on a rock ledge, and stayed in the nook to catch his breath.

After his breathing and the pounding of his heart both leveled out, Pierce heard the shriek of the T-Rex topside. It stomped its feet in anger, and then stalked the jungle for its next meal. Pierce had escaped certain death once again.

Willy, the cannibals, the dinosaurs, the secrets of the island, they all repeated in his dizzy and tired mind. They paraded around in his skull to remind him he didn't stand a chance of getting off of this island alive. Whatever Lee Branch had come here to investigate, the man knew very little of the truths that existed on the island.

The next step was hard to determine. He needed food and water, and quick, or he'd die before making any real attempt at tracking down Susan.

"There's nobody here to help you," Skeeter said. "I respect you as a private investigator. You could solve any case, but you're not a mercenary. Angel wanted you to be like us. She never told you that. She had you tag along on all of those expeditions in the chance you might become interested in our work. But you can't be something you're not. No matter how hard you try."

Hard Case gave Pierce his two cents next. "Skeeter's right. You're not a mercenary. You learned a few things, sure, but it takes more than guts and balls and insanity to do what we do. You have to have that killer instinct, and you either have it or you don't. You don't have it, Pierce. Angel couldn't get over it. She refused to quit trying. She loved you that much. She didn't want to leave you, even if your relationship was doomed to fail."

Shark spoke up. "None of us were married for a reason. Think about it, Pierce. Our job isn't safe. Our income comes at random times. We disappear for weeks at a time. You can't start a family like that. Angel thought she could do both with you, but she kept forgetting you can't be a mercenary and a mom. It doesn't work. She tried. She refused to give up, the poor bitch."

"She loved me," Pierce argued. "It could've worked; we could've kept trying. We were happy. She would've been my wife if she hadn't died."

"Yeah, keep telling yourself that," Shark said. "It never would've worked anyway."

"One day," Hard Case said, "she would've had to end it. Deny it all you want."

Skeeter went for the throat. "It doesn't matter. She's dead, you're going to be dead, so why think about such things?"

Pierce's blood boiled. He flew into a rage. "Fuck you all! Why do I keep seeing you people? Get out of my head! Get the fuck out of my head!!!"

Pierce was sobbing hard. He couldn't get over Angel. They would've made it work. They loved each other. But it didn't matter. She *was* dead. Burned up in the plane wreck, and gone forever.

The real issue was the most complex.

How could he move on with his life after Angel died?

The grief came to him in a flood.

"I have to stop feeling sorry for myself. This isn't the right way to deal with grief. I can't keep talking to dead people. It's not healthy. It's not sane. Get out of my head, and stay out of my head. I have to take this island on my way."

The mercenaries vanished.

Angel appeared for a moment before hiding into the abyss of Pierce's mind.

"You're right, Pierce. You must solve your own problems now. It doesn't mean I don't love you. You must find Susan, and somehow stay alive."

When Angel disappeared, Pierce sobbed some more before falling into an exhausted sleep.

Fever Dreams

Pierce suffered fever dreams. He relived parts of his life in an overwhelming onslaught of horror. Pierce was surrounded by flames as he turned over the pieces of a wrecked plane. The flesh on his arms and back were singed. The rage of flames intensified, as did the pain of first-degree burns advancing into second degree. He kept digging and digging, and all he came up with was more flames, and gasoline-soaked wreckage. Angel was in there somehow, buried. Pierce kept burning, and burning, and burning until he looked down at both of his hands. They were bared to blackened skeleton.

Then Pierce was in an empty boxcar. He was checking out leads on a case as a private detective. Pierce was supposed to track Sarah Paulson's husband to determine if he was cheating on her. He followed Mr. Paulson to an empty boxcar in the downtown part of the city. It was then Pierce realized the figure was actually Sarah Paulson, dressed in a trench coat inside the boxcar. When Pierce entered the boxcar, she was undressing herself down to nothing. Sarah tweaked her nipple, and threw her head back to tempt the detective into a fling. The whole job had been a sexual game for Sarah. Her husband wasn't cheating on her. She was cheating on him. This much had happened in real life, but what the fever dream added was the heart beating on the outside of her body. The muscle pumped fresh spurts of hot blood down her naked breasts and body.

Pierce was thrown from that horrible vision to another. He was knocking on a door belonging to an apartment building. His job was to locate a missing teenager for two concerned parents. They weren't sure if she was a runaway, or if she had been abducted by somebody four days ago. Pierce was tracing her last steps, and was about to talk to the missing girl's boyfriend, when the door he was about to knock on shot open. It was Willy, and he lunged for Pierce. Both hands were wrapped around Pierce's throat. He couldn't breathe. The life was slowly leaving him as every process in his body was constricted.

"Choke and die! Nobody one-ups Willy! Nobody nobody nobody!"

Pierce removed his .38 pistol from his holster, and emptied bullet after bullet after bullet into Willy's midsection. Willy only laughed as his guts were torn up by hot lead.

"You can't kill ol' Willy! I'm going to choke you to death, and then I'm going to feed you to those cannibals! Fresh meat! I'll cut your dick off, and feed it to them! Then your balls. I can't wait to hear them pop in their mouths!"

Still choking, everything was going dim in Pierce's eyes. All he could see were crosscuts of Willy's face in the darkness. Somewhere, a light beam half-painted the madman's face. From a flashlight maybe, he thought. Pierce wasn't sure what to make of it, he was paralyzed under the powerful weight of Willy's body. No way to save himself. Both of Willy's hands squeezed so hard Pierce thought the man meant to rip off his head.

"Maybe I won't feed you to the cannibals," Willy rasped. "There are no rules here on this island. A body's a body, right? A shame to waste it. A man can do a lot with a corpse. I like to play games. Yeah...I think I'll keep your corpse, Pierce. I'll invade every part of you before I feed you to the things out there."

When Willy shouted "YES! DIE!" The man's eyeball fired out of the socket like a bullet from a pop gun. The eyeball did three bounces, and dangled on a pink string. Willy released Pierce's throat. Pierce surged awake from his dream state.

But it wasn't a dream state!

Pierce was sucking in air to save his life for real. Thinking fast, he located a loose rock, and smashed it against the side of Willy's head. Willy was still balancing the orb with two hands when the stone's blow forced him through the wall of falling water. Willy splashed down into the water on the other side.

Pierce located the source of light: an industrial flashlight. He picked it up, and moved to the side of the waterfall to look out at the water. He scanned the light in every direction. Willy was gone. He couldn't believe how close he came to dying.

You have to snap out of it. You can't go to pieces now. There has to be more people like Willy out there. It's not safe. Get your head out of your ass.

Pure darkness painted the jungle. He clutched the flashlight, but what good would that be in finding food and water? Whether it be Willy, or some other psycho who worked on the island, or the jungle itself, he was in the crosshairs of everything.

Pierce listened to the water crash down. He heard nothing from Willy. Pierce wasn't sure what to do now in the dark of night. It wasn't until he turned around that the light caught something very important.

A Helpful Clue

The wadded up hiking pack was covered in splashes of dried up blood, but that didn't stop Pierce from searching its contents. He located a canteen of water and drank gratefully from it. He also located a protein bar, and ate it slowly so as not to make himself sick. The food and water lifted his spirits instantly. There was a pair of binoculars and a pad of paper. He searched the pad of paper, reading the pages of notations about the island. It didn't take long for Pierce to realize this was Lee Branch's hiking pack.

The notebook explained how Lee's boat was attacked by masked individuals who gunned down his crew. Lee was alone, and his boat was sailing through fog aimlessly until he reached the island. Lee escaped a group of persons who tried to take him captive. He was attacked by everything Pierce had experienced so far. The last page was the sketch of a crude map. It showed Pierce's position at the waterfall. If he went down a trail headed east for a mile, he would run smack into an electrified fence that led into a base.

In the notes, Lee described the base as an unknown place of operations. What, or who, resided in the building, Lee couldn't say. The man had guesses. They were living quarters for the workers who maintained and secured the island. It was also a business office and a facility that dumped and stored illegal chemicals on the island. Whatever else went on here, Lee wanted to find out.

Judging by the blood on the pack, Lee was located before he could answer any of the questions on his mind.

Where did Lee and Susan get their information on the island? He didn't remember Susan ever telling him their source. Pierce couldn't help but think this was a trap for groups who might get caught up in their illegal business. From what Susan told him, the bottom of The Green Project was starting to give. The cause was near its breaking point. This secret island had the backing of some very powerful people who would love for The Green Project to be terminated.

What am I supposed to do against them? Pierce thought. The enormity of the problem for one man was impossible to dissect in his present situation.

I can't expose what's happening here. That's the thing. Let's pretend you locate Susan, get the hell off of this island, and somehow return home. Who would we tell that could help us? There would be so many roadblocks and assassins out there to keep the island a secret. You will never see the end of it until they kill you.

No, I can't leave this island. I can't run away and live happily ever after. That's been squashed.

Okay, I can't run from them. I have to destroy their base. I have to make it impossible for them to come after me.

I have to take out everything on this island.

Skeeter, Shark, and Hard Case appeared in the flashlight's glow. They didn't say a word. This time, they regarded Pierce with respect. They agreed with Pierce's assessment.

Every bad guy had to die.

Pierce drank more water and allowed enough time for his body to recharge before he set out with the flashlight. He followed Lee's map to the perimeter fence.

Path in the Dark

The night was active with strange jungle noises. Pierce knew there were dinosaurs and cannibals out there waiting for the right opportunity to devour his ass. He didn't use the flashlight. Instead, he allowed his eyes to adjust to the darkness enough so that he could take a slow trek to his destination.

Pierce stopped and stayed low to the ground. He crouched behind a tree when he heard the sound of tires rolling. The vehicle stopped about twenty yards ahead of him. The jeep's headlights painted the jungle with blue-white light, and the two men in painter's suits were combing the area with a giant spotlight. They were talking about Pierce, then their talk strayed to Willy.

"Willy hasn't reported back in an hour. Either he's playing with himself, or the asshole got himself eaten. Wouldn't be the first time we lost one of our best in something's stomach.

"Hey, if we have time, you know where that velociraptor's nest is? We should set it on fire. Or how about we shock the shit out of the un-hatched eggs with electricity until they explode? That passes the long nights."

"There's time for that shit later. We need to find that guy on the run. He's out there somewhere."

"Unless he got eaten."

"Willy reported having seen the intruder near here. The bastard wouldn't say where, he wanted the guy to himself. Willy's probably just having himself a good old time while we're busting out backs trying to track down his ass."

"We can have fun too. Fuck Willy. Let's blow up some eggs."

"You know what? You're right. We deserve some fun too."

Pierce crouched lower to the earth when the light crossed over near where he hid. The light continued without stopping. After five more minutes, the two henchmen revved up their jeep, and drove somewhere else.

Pierce didn't waste a single moment. He kept moving in the direction the map instructed. Pierce was surprised how it was only a matter of minutes before the jungle thinned out, and he stood in front of the fence lined with barbed wire.

He could hear the hum of electricity.

Pierce couldn't jump the fence or cut the wire.

"Nice try," Skeeter said. "Looks like your plan to save the day has already collapsed."

Shark was meaner. "You could never be a mercenary. Sure, you're a private dick who can dig in trashcans and take pictures of cheating husbands, but you're no warrior. You're not a real man. Nice try. I'm sure if Angel was still around, she'd do it for you."

Hard Case agreed. "She always had bigger balls than you, man. I bet when you guys screwed, she was always on top. I bet you took it real good."

Pierce was breathing harder. His blood flowed fast with pent up rage. Pierce refused to bottle it up any longer.

"Why the fuck are you here? I'm tired of seeing you assholes. I'm only trying to do the right thing. Fuck you! I don't need you anymore. I don't want to die anymore, you hear me? I'm willing to fight for what's right. You haven't done a damn thing to help me. Angel's gone, and there's no bringing her back. I have to wake up and face reality. It wasn't my fault I couldn't save her, I nearly burned to death trying to rescue her. It's not my fault. I can't have her because she's gone, but it doesn't mean I have to die too!"

The mercenaries vanished. Then Angel appeared. She smiled at him. Tears gleamed in her eyes. "You finally said what you needed to say, Pierce. I'll always love you. Never forget that. Now go save Susan. I'll always be with you, but you're on your own now. Start a new life. You only live once, Pierce."

Angel drew him close, kissed him real hard like a lover, and disappeared.

Pierce had to take in the moment before returning to reality.

He stood in front of the fence with the night sounds of the jungle filling up the air with deadly possibilities.

The problem remained the same.

How could he save Susan?

Better yet, how was he going to get over the fence without frying his ass?

Pierce took several steps back to get a wider view of the fence. Beyond the barrier, he could see lights on inside the brick buildings.

All you have to do is get through that fence, and you can really start looking for answers.

Pierce was going to walk along the fence border and search for any breaks or ideas, when his foot hit something. He stubbed his toe. A surge of pain crawled up his foot like a hot coil.

Whatever it was, it was rock solid.

Pierce picked up a giant bone from a dinosaur. He clutched what looked to be a femur bone for several seconds before it hit him. He was on the ground on all fours, working like a wild man to get the job done. It would take hours to complete the job, Pierce knew, but he didn't care. He was going to dig under the fence to get to the other side.

Part Two: Susan's Big Day

Meet the Man

Susan Branch was standing naked in front of a mirror. The room was the size of a mall's changing room. She was covered in mean bruises along her arms where the hideous men had dragged her from the boat and forced her to hike three miles to their base. Susan could still see the henchmen's unnatural deformity. One man had no skull or skin along his forehead. She could see the man's glistening brains right through a sheath of active mucus. The other goon had two heads. The second head was poorly formed. Its head flesh was the color of a dirty root. The eyes were bloody cherries, and the lips were leathery meat. The head didn't speak, it drooled. The goons had delivered her through several empty hallways with closed off rooms to take her to this small chamber. There, she was told to change into new clothes. Those new clothes were a thin cloth hospital gown that tied at the back and a pair of shoes. She was a captive prisoner. What that truly meant, she would soon find out.

They told Susan to open the door after she had changed, so she opened the door and stood there. Only one of the goons remained in the hallway. That was the two-headed goon wearing a dark blue painter's uniform. He held an electric shock prod in one hand and a leather leash with a studded collar in the other.

On the man's breast, it read "Joey."

The gnarly root head didn't have a name.

"I'm going to put this on your neck, Mrs. Branch. You don't like it, take it up with the boss. Care to take it up with me, I'll jam this shock rod up your ass. My other head wants me to stick it up somewhere else. He's into that kinky shit. Who knows what I'll do when the time comes? If you want to find out, try me, lady."

Susan didn't say a word.

Joey slipped the leather collar around Susan's neck. The goon gripped the leash in his free hand. "Okay, Mrs. Branch. You walk in front of me. Keep a nice pace. Don't try anything funny." He pressed a button on the shock prod. It crackled with a fresh burst of electricity. "Or this goes inside of you. Tell me you understand, and you will obey. Say those exact words, Mrs. Branch."

"I understand," Susan said nervously. "I will obey."

"Very good," Joey said. "Both of us like you very much. I think we'll later become better acquainted. Second head thinks you're very pretty...and I think the same."

Gee thanks, you sick fuck. I'm so honored.

Susan knew she was alone in this endeavor. Her father explained how these people were nothing more than criminals, and would conduct themselves in a lawless manner. Whatever illegal work occurred on this island, these henchmen were given a certain freedom to do as they wished. That included doing heinous things to the people they held captive.

She had to start thinking about protecting herself. Nobody was here to save her. Pierce Range was dead. He was the first to go down. Pierce was a beacon of false hope; he had disappointed her. Three years ago, Susan thought he was bulletproof, the way he dispatched her kidnappers. That didn't hold true to the present.

Pierce is no better than a washed up drunk.

I can't believe I thought he could help us.

The rest of the team fared no better. Joey and his henchmen friend sent Lords, Staff, and Berkley loose on the island. Joey said they were heading straight to the cannibal area. Whatever that meant, Susan still didn't know. The henchmen only laughed as the members of The Green Project faced certain death.

Susan was taking steps down a hallway now. Everything was clean and sterile. The screams from the other rooms was disconcerting. They weren't human screams. Susan couldn't pinpoint what could've made those horrible sounds. They were high pitched, and unleashing levels of pain unknown to her life's experience.

"You're wondering what those noises are coming from outside? Call it our second security system. Sure, we have an electrified fence around our base, but this is more of a psychological attack on our enemies. What you're hearing are the tortured screams of dinosaurs. We've got areas outside the base designated to showcase our superiority."

Susan was afraid to say the man was crazy, and that dinosaurs were long ago extinct. What she was hearing could've easily represented a tortured monster's plea for it all to end, but she refused to believe what the man was telling her.

"You don't believe me," Joey laughed. "You haven't seen them, so you won't believe me until you do. You'll see plenty of evidence on the tour. Don't you worry."

The tour?

Now Susan was nervous. What did they have in store for her? They knew she was the daughter of Lee Branch. The island didn't like trespassers, especially the environmentalist kind. So, what would her future hold at this savage island?

This wasn't a protest against organizations that destroyed nature.

This was now a fight to save her life.

Susan continued down the hallway until they stopped in front of a set of double doors that led outside. Around those doors was a lobby area; this seemed to be the entrance to the base. Along the walls were stuffed mounts.

Human heads.

"Ah, you're noticing my accomplishments!" A jovial voice greeted her from another outlet of the hallway. This man stood six feet tall. He was a built two hundred and fifty pounds of pure muscle and force. The mysterious man wore a red silk cloth that covered his face from the nose down to his chin. "Welcome to my island, Mrs. Branch. Now father and daughter can be reunited. First, I wanted to give you a tour of the base."

The man patted Joey on the back. "Good work, Joey. I can always depend on you to get results."

Joey smiled big. "Thanks, boss."

The second head tried to shape a smile, and only unleashed a thick stream of drool down its chin.

"Forgive me, Mrs. Branch," the man said in a deep voice. Susan imagined a human lion talking, his voice was so deep. "I haven't introduced myself. I could tell you my real name, but I prefer the title I've been given by environmental organizations like yours. You can call me Hangman."

"I understand your silence," Hangman went on. "So let me do the talking. If you have questions or comments, please, feel free to speak. Joey won't shock you. He'll only give you the juice if you try to run."

Hangman pointed at the two dozen mounted heads on the wall. "You've got men and women from across the globe. All environmentalists, crusaders of nature, and brave souls who dared to go against the way of industry and commerce. They protest, they picket, they sabotage, and they expose our operations. We do the world's dirty work, and this is the thanks we get?

"I cut their heads off myself, Mrs. Branch, with an axe. Let me be clear. I will always win. You can stall my operation, you can throw a wrench in the machine, but that's all that will happen. You can't win. We're too big and powerful for anybody to stop. And still, little brave souls like you keep poking around in our business.

"Lessons must be learned, and I'm the one to dole out the punishments. You see, I was hired by Globo Corps to run this island. It's a funny story. This island had been uninhabited since the beginning of time...so Globo Corps thought. Go back about twenty years, and Globo Corps flies out payloads of chemicals from hundreds of manufacturing companies. Think battery factories, pharmaceutical leftovers, hazardous waste from hospitals and cancer research facilities, and the general toxic and biohazard shit that modern life has created. Globo Corps flew big helicopters, and simply dumped the shit on the island.

"The problem was, Globo Corps didn't realize tribes of people live on this island, as do dinosaurs. Dinosaurs, right? I mean, what an oversight! This island's been untouched since the beginning of time. The land is constantly surrounded by a ring of fog that spans for miles and miles in every direction. Maybe that was nature's way of keeping its secrets. Well, fuck nature. God created humans that were superior to dirt, rocks, and trees, so onward with progress. Am I right?

"We cure diseases, and increase the world's technology. Of course, some unintended messes are going to occur. So what? This island will do its job as long as people like me, Joey, and the others are here to police it.

"You're probably wondering who would take on such a job? Everybody here has been trained and recruited from prisons. Think about the numbers of people who've been put on death row, or were sentenced to life terms. Not everybody's cut out for this work, even though the reward is high. You'll learn firsthand what that means, Mrs. Branch.

"Anyway, I'm going on and on. Let's begin the tour. I can't wait to show you what this island has to offer."

Hangman's Tour

Outside those double doors was a courtyard. There were no trees or special foliage, only an odd pile of bones. She thought it was a post-modern sculpture until she noticed the long reptilian skulls and bones that were well beyond the size of any humans or animal's. They looked to be dinosaur bones. The bones were wrapped up in barbed wire. A bronze plaque was placed below the bones. The inscription read: *Man Conquers All*.

Susan thought back to the mounted human's heads, and the explanation Hangman offered about the island. She couldn't help but ask her captor the question.

"You set my dad up, didn't you? You gave him the directions to the island. You were the tipster."

Susan couldn't see Hangman's expressions beneath the red silk cloth. His delight showed in those devilish eyes. "Smart girl, aren't you? Yes, I was the one who reached out to your father. I put out the bait, and he ate it right up. That's what Globo Corps does. Instead of going after their enemies, they trick them into coming here. They either get eaten up by the dinosaurs, thrown onto a cannibal's plate, or we get our hands on them. Joey likes it when we capture them alive, don't you, Joey?"

Joey's eyes doubled. "Yes, sir."

The second head managed a smile without drooling this time.

"Our goal is to hunt down our enemies until they're no more," Hangman said. "Maybe one day, those who think of acting like nature's ambassadors will think twice and start minding their own business. We've pretty much dismantled The Green Project. Now that's something to celebrate."

Hangman motioned for Joey to lead Susan to the jeep parked nearby. Joey loaded her up into the backseat and sat right next to her, while Hangman took the wheel. Hangman had a walkie and called up to the guard's tower that stood tall beside the large steel barrier entrance. "Open the gates."

There was a crackle on the line, and then someone spoke, "You got it, sir."

The gates opened. They were driving down a dirt path along a grassy straightaway. Barbed fences at least thirty feet high surrounded them.

"I keep a long open area around our compound in case intruders dare to cross the electrified fences. They'll be easy to stop out in the open. Nowhere to hide. Snipers can blow their heads rights off."

Hangman kept driving. Another fence perimeter appeared. Men in dark blue suits worked to open the gates securely. Susan saw a few of them, and their abnormalities. One of them had three arms on one side of him. He used one arm to open the fence, while the other two clutched onto sub-machine guns. Another guard had a hand dangling from his chin. The guard saw Susan staring at him, and the hand flipped her off.

"They don't like it when you stare too long, Mrs. Branch," Joey said. "But you can look at me as long as you like. I don't mind a woman's eyes on me."

Oh Jesus.

Hangman laughed. "Joey sure enjoys his women. Who doesn't? Especially when they're all as pretty as you, Mrs. Branch. I think we're all going to enjoy you very much. We'll make you last."

That burning hot coil of fear burned up her spine. There was no doubt as to what things these awful people had planned for her. Susan refused to buckle under the stress. There had to be a way out of this, and she prayed to God there was an escape.

The fence opened up. The jeep drove forward, staying on a dirt path cut out from the thick jungle. Susan thought of the many places she could run and hide. What prevented her from diving out of the vehicle was the leather dog's leash on her neck. If she jumped from the jeep, it was probable she would snap her neck.

Susan didn't have much time to consider any options of escape.

The jeep soon stopped.

Up ahead was a destination spot on Hangman's tour.

A Horrific Show

When the jeep stopped, Hangman didn't say a single word. Joey and his head observed the area with pride. Susan had to deal with two realities at once. One, that dinosaurs did in fact exist, and two, those creatures were being tormented. A series of iron cages were spread out in a box cut out of the jungle. Two raptors were trapped in one iron-barred cage. One raptor had turned against the other and was eating from a half-rotten carcass. A brontosaurus was left out in direct sunlight to bake in the sun. The dinosaur lay on its side, slowly dying. The body was deflated leather. The other cages housed various types of dinosaurs, all trapped in cages without food, or trapped with another of its kind so they would eat the other. Hanging from the nearby trees were dinosaur body parts hanging from rope. The smell surrounding the area was an offensive wall of fecundity. The sight and smell coupled together to force Susan to lean over the edge of the jeep and lose her stomach. Joey had to give her slack on the leash. When she came back up, Hangman drove on from the horrible place of death.

"We have to make the dinosaurs fear us," Hangman explained. "If we don't, they'll kill us all. They might be lower thinking creatures, but they're smart enough to fear pain, and to recognize those who can inflict it. This show of brutality is a requirement. Considering our efforts, we still lose men doing their everyday jobs to dinosaur attacks."

The jeep continued down the trail.

Susan couldn't believe her eyes.

Something horrible was coming right their way.

"Don't worry, I'm hitting the gas," Hangman said. "This is a normal occurrence on this island. The mutations, I mean."

A blanketing wall of flies the size of softballs buzzed towards them. The flies were hundreds thick. Joey got up, let go of her leash, and picked up a long gun that looked like a rocket launcher. White smoke sprayed out the tip. The flies were immediately hit by the smoke and abruptly turned the other way. Susan thought about leaping out of the jeep, but Hangman had reached around, and had his hand on her leg.

"Repellant does the job," Hangman said. "We got giant flies, rhinoceros beetles that are big enough to eat dogs, and look up ahead! There they are. Our friendly neighbors. Say hello!"

Susan went from one mode of disgust, to an even higher level of shock. Human bones were stacked up into a tall hill. Beyond that hill were straw huts. Susan caught sight of a crude stage for killing. People dressed in loincloths and painted in strange symbols danced around at their presence. They clutched onto sharpened wood spears and wood axes, but didn't dare come close to the jeep.

The longer she studied the group, Susan noticed their freak abnormalities. A few had multiple limbs, or two heads, like Joey, and many had organs pumping with life on the outside of their bodies. The worse example she saw was a woman with a liver and spleen on top of her head. It bisected her facial features, creating a hideous expression. Susan had to turn away with tears in her eyes.

This place is so wrong.

Susan's feelings didn't change when her eyes happened upon the ground heaped in spread out intestines, and chunks of broken bones. People were savagely killed here. These people were not only the victims of contamination, they were real-life cannibals. She knew this because there was torn clothing belonging to her team spread out about the area. Lords, Staff, and Berkley were savagely murdered and devoured here.

Hangman removed a .38 special from his hip holster and rattled off five rounds into the air. The cannibals were jolted by the noises and fled into a hole in the ground for safety. "*Yeaaaaaaaaaaah!* Run, you stupid pieces of shit. Go into your hidey-hole. Know your place, you stinking rats.

"Not only do we have to suppress the dinosaurs, these cannibals can keep our hands full too. We have to actively show our dominance in order to maintain the safety of our staff. It's not easy.

"By the way, I'm not giving you this tour for kicks. You must understand there is no escape. If you run out there, know you're throwing yourself into a worse situation than what we could ever muster. The tour is to back up what I'm saying. You're ours, totally and completely. Do as we say, and you might get to live. We even have a few ladies who enjoy it here. They treat us real good. When they treat us real good, we tend to reciprocate."

Hangman told her they had one more stop on the tour before he got to show her something extra special. What "extra special" could mean made her stomach churn in miserable anticipation.

Dumping Ground

Susan couldn't see it, but she could smell it. She imagined burning plastic, boiling bleach, nose-pinching sulfur, and melting Styrofoam. Billowing clouds of gray and white smoke rose up from a circle in the near distance. Iron gates surrounded the perimeter of the pollution box. The jeep stopped outside the main gates. The armed guards in two towers studied them. Hangman waved for them to go about their duty. Susan could see tall steel vats and storage tanks. Between steel pipes connecting everything, steam snuck out of cracks in the steel, as did occasional neon green drips. Workers wearing Hazmat suits and gas masks were checking gauges, core temperatures, and patching up the leaks from the hundreds of storage tanks.

"You see, inside the area we process what is brought to the island. An aircraft will drop the payload from the sky. Our boys collect it, process it in our facility, maintain these corrosive elements, and keep them as far away from humanity as possible. We're doing a wonderful service here. The problem, sometimes we have serious leaks, and this hazardous stuff leeches into the drinking water. We've had mutations, and I, for one, am not a stranger to mutation."

Hangman pointed to the red silk kerchief covering his lower face.

"I have sacrificed as much as our workers have. We do this without thanks or an end to our duties. We do this because our country has called upon us to continue this burdensome task. It's the cost of being an American. Some Americans pay a higher price than others for their freedom. Know it as a way of life, Mrs. Branch."

Susan couldn't change who she was, and that was an environmentalist. She bled green. Hangman could spout justifications for this island all he wanted, but she smelled bullshit over the sulfur.

"All of you have hearts of gold. You're hiding illegal chemicals for illegal big businesses. Let's wave the American flag in your honor. Hypocrites. You're contaminating the life on this island. You're contaminating yourselves. I don't care if that tribe back there is a cannibal tribe, and who knows, maybe these chemicals turned them into cannibals, but they didn't ask for us to come to their home and wreck everything. It starts here, but where does it end? If what you're doing is so innocent, why are you doing this in secrecy? Why kill those who stumble upon the truth? Your ideology is full of gaping holes."

Hangman didn't have anything to say, except, "Sometimes you have to wake up and realize you have to pick a side. I pick the side that's in power. You picked the losing side, Mrs. Branch. Remember that during your stay here on my island; keep telling yourself what you need to tell yourself to get through life, and I'll do the same for myself. Now there's one more thing to show you, and that will bring a conclusion to the tour."

The Special Surprise

Dread welled up into Susan's stomach. Her insides were that of a boiling vat of illegal chemicals. What did Hangman have in store for her next? The way Joey and his second head ogled her bare thighs sticking out of the paper-thin gown clued her in. She had to keep telling herself she was full of fight, piss and vinegar, and a stomp your enemies into the ground mentality.

Did Hangman have a point earlier? He picked the winning side, and Susan, well, she was on the side that was always a half step behind the opposition. The Green Project was as good as finished. She was one person working for a dead organization.

Where did that leave Susan?

Dead.

The ride was a backtrack of the previous tour. The cannibal tribe was still hiding underground. Susan was jolted by the sound of a skull being crushed under the front tire.

Joey said, "It's okay. Just be glad it's not your skull, Mrs. Branch. Yours is still in your head."

They returned to the tortured dinosaurs in cages. The dinosaurs that were alive, and had enough energy to show a reaction, cowered in fear as the jeep headed back to the main base. Through the main gates, they traveled back to where they had started from.

Joey guided her by the dog leash through the main doors. Hangman walked five paces ahead of them. He couldn't wait to show Susan the surprise. Susan lowered her head viewing the mounted heads on the wall. She recognized Joyce Merryweather and Howard Best, both from The Green Project, who had saved over a dozen species of animals from going extinct, and had worked tirelessly in third world countries to deliver malaria nets, clean drinking water, medical aid, and contraception education. What had Joyce and Howard done to land in the crosshairs of Hangman? It sounded like this organization targeted environmentalist groups like terrorists targeted innocent people. They did it all to spread fear into their enemies.

Susan had to ask herself, had anyone truly spread fear into Hangman's operation here on the island? She snarled thinking about it. It was about time somebody gave Hangman a dose of his own medicine.

Up ahead, Hangman hit a button to open up an elevator.

"We're headed down," Hangman said. "Brace yourself, Susan."

Susan had no idea how to do such a thing in a place like this.

She did everything to busy her mind during the elevator ride down. She counted four floors on the button panel. Hangman had pressed two buttons. Level 2 and Level 3. Joey appeared to be startled by the fact Hangman had done so.

Hangman anticipated Joey's apprehension.

"You're due for your weekly physical," Hangman said to Joey. "I know you don't like your visits with the doctor. Dr. Prater does his best to make them as quick and painless as possible. When you run an operation with a staff of mutants, you've got to twist their fucking arms to get them through the doctor's door. I feel your pain, Joey. I have to look at myself in the mirror everyday. I'm just like all of you. Prolonged exposure to this chemical shit does it to you. Now you know why we can't leave this island. The world will never accept us. This island is where we belong. We've talked about this during the staff meetings. Do we need to have that talk again?"

Joey tensed his grip on Susan's leash. "*No*. I understand. This is where I belong. My family is here. My friends are here. My life is here."

Susan could see terror on Joey's second head. And were those tears in both of their eyes?

The elevator opened to the second floor.

"I'll take the leash, Joey," Hangman said. "Now go on. Let Dr. Prater look you over."

The area outside the elevator was the furthest thing from a doctor's waiting room. Dozens of men in those greasy painter's suits stood in place with their heads down. A rope cordoned a long line leading into the doctor's office. Whatever was beyond those double doors, Susan knew it brought tension and fear into the workers.

Susan had trouble meeting the eyes of those in line. She saw a woman whose face was covered in dozens of eyes, a bared sinus cavity for a nose, and a lipless mouth. Another man's face had melted, making it look like a surface of melting candle waxberries. He had a mouth at his throat, and a single eyeball peering out of what used to be a chin. Others were equally as disfigured by exposure to hazardous materials.

Joey entered the room with his head down, and stepped into the line.

The elevator closed.

Hangman sighed. "I feel for them. I meet with Dr. Prater as often as they do. Our bodies are affected by this island, as you can see. Sometimes we need corrective surgeries, and Dr. Prater is a genius when it comes to skin grafts, transplants, and cancer removals. We have to keep our workers going, and when they need modifications, it can be quite painful. We don't always have narcotics on hand, so..."

"Do you ever go under the knife without narcotics?" Susan dared to ask. Why did Hangman feel the need to justify the scene when she hadn't said a single word? She knew how these bastards functioned and survived their day-to-day life. They fed themselves bullshit lies and believed every syllable as truth.

Hangman huffed, turned his head to the side, and didn't reply.

The time stretched on as the elevator counted down to level one. When the elevator opened, Susan faced a narrow walkway.

She imagined a poorly kept police station. The walls were bare wood. The ceiling had exposed light fixtures. The incandescent beams were over bright. Worse yet were the orange-brown spatters on every surface.

Blood spatters.

How many people were forced down these halls and beaten? The doors were made of solid steel. Perfect for entrapment. She heard people wailing in pain. The sharp cracking of whips. The dripping of water as somebody was being water boarded. Steel instruments scraped against bone. A man was verbally grilling somebody as they cried and begged for understanding. Susan caught a partially open door where five of the henchmen were savagely beating a man who was naked and covered in blood and bruises. Another room, she caught a man being injected with truth serum. A man in scrubs was checking the needle and I.V., while another asked questions and wrote down things on a notepad. A different room had a long window showing a series of large wooden boxes. A henchmen was walking by, rapping a club against the boxes, and laughing his head off. Susan knew people were in those boxes. It was another form of torture. In other corners, people were standing on platforms with their arms tied up over their heads. How many hours had they stood there in anguish?

Susan lost her spine in that moment. Having a fight or flight attitude meant nothing here. They were in control. These horrible people had the numbers, the evil inside them, and the full, unchecked capabilities of turning one's sanity inside out, and shitting on their souls.

She was losing feeling in her body. Everything was going numb. Hangman kept guiding her on by the dog leash through various rooms turned into cages and torture chambers. The area changed from torture chambers to prison cells. Steel doors kept their inhabitants a secret. New smells hit her in the face: shit, blood, sweat, and piss, and a sharp chemical smell, like burnt plastic and bleach met with something that made the face and throat sting. She was breathing in noxious fumes. It was making her dizzy. Her steps were wobbly.

"Almost there," Hangman said, tugging back on her leash. "Two more doors, and we're there. Hang on, Ms. Branch."

Hangman was behind her now, holding her up so she couldn't tip over and crash to the ground. They closed in on a single steel door. When Hangman opened the door, he also removed the collar and forced Susan through the threshold.

Before the door closed, Hangman laughed under his breath, and said, "I'll give you a few minutes to catch up with your father. I'm sure Lee will be happy to see his daughter again."

Hangman gave her one hard push before shutting the door. Susan landed on her knees. The sharp pain in her bones woke her from that chemical fog.

The cell wasn't very big. It barely held one person, a cot, and a toilet. The walls were a drab gray color. She imagined the color of a nail's head. Someone could easily lose their sanity in such a place.

The person who occupied the cell with her wasn't familiar at first. Who could recognize anybody who had undergone such a hideous transformation? She imagined a man whose skin had melted like wax, then hardened, and stayed that way permanently. All of his features had sagged, creating an exaggerated expression of sadness. The man couldn't wear clothing, except white pants made out of a plastic material.

"Dad...is that you?"

Her voice was choked with tears. She reached out to hold him, but Lee told her to stay away.

"My nerves are exposed," Lee growled. "Every moment I stand here in the open air is agony. I've had chemicals and pollutants injected into me intravenously. They've perfected mutation on human subjects. They take people out of prisons, inject them with shit, and put them to work. It all adds up to instant enslavement."

Susan told her father she loved him, and what monsters Hangman and the people on this island were. Lee didn't hear a word of it.

Lee had a message of his own to relay.

"I waited for you, Susan. I have a plan to save you now that you're here. I knew they'd bring you here, otherwise, I would've chewed my wrists open and killed myself by now. My God, the pain is so unbearable. But this isn't about me anymore. It's about preserving the cause. If it's my dying act to keep The Green Project a reality, then so be it."

Lee put his hands into hers and whispered, "I know they're going to put you down in the basement in a cage. Don't be scared. Whatever they threaten you with, I'll protect you. I have a plan. You'll know when I've started that plan. *Just wait for the screaming to start.*"

Before Susan could say something else, Hangman re-entered the cell. He hooked the dog leash back onto the collar at her neck.

"I see father and daughter environmentalist have been reacquainted. You didn't bother giving daddy a kiss on his melted cheese mouth. Don't feel bad, Susan. I wouldn't pucker up to that hot pizza face in a million years.

"But you, Susan, have quite a body on you. You'll be wonderful to boost morale here on the island. Just as often as we have to keep our employees subservient, we have to justify our cause with reward. Your sweet ass is that reward. And know this, Lee, I'll be the first to taste your daughter's sweetness. Then the others will turn her inside out until she's so used up, I'll throw her to the cannibals. If they don't rape her to death, they'll at least eat the meat from her bones.

"Know this. As long as Globo Corps tells me to keep this island running, nobody will ever stop us. It's good this island's here. Eager environmentalists like yourselves will keep sticking their necks out when I dangle the bait in front of their faces. They'll keep coming right to me, and I'll keep killing them."

Hangman threw his head back and unleashed his evil laugh. Then Susan was out of the cell. Hangman kept jerking back on the leash. Soon, she was back in the elevator.

I know they're going to put you down in the basement in a cage.

Lee promised to protect her.

That gave her a shred of hope.

As the elevator ticked down to the basement level, Susan remembered her father's instructions.

All she had to do was wait for the screaming to start to be saved.

The Basement Level

The elevator stopped at the basement level. Hangman kept the elevator doors from opening and gave Susan a final warning. "I know the condition of your father may come as a shock to you. I've merely been building up your tolerance for the unbelievable things coming your way. My enemies can't think I'm going soft on anybody, male or female, pretty or not. They're going to pick on you down here. My men, after a long hard day of working with the risks surrounding them here on the island, they sure like to take out their frustrations on a nice piece of ass. You're the nicest, newest piece we've come across in awhile now, Susan. I won't lie and say you'll one day survive this and be set free, because you won't. You will die here. How you'll die will remain a mystery. You'll either die of exhaustion, internal bleeding, contamination, infection, or you'll simply will yourself to die like a few of our previous members have. Your father can't save you. And you should thank me for letting you see him one more time. Most people in my position wouldn't even give you that. Remember that when it's my turn with you in the luxury suite."

Hangman pressed the button that opened the elevator doors without another word. He guided her down to what resembled a prison. Iron-barred cells were lined up together so far back she couldn't see the end of them. Men and women wore tatters and rags for clothes. They were covered in bruises, exhausted, beaten, and ruined of will. Susan could see it, smell it, and sense the heavy burden of broken hope in the air. Some, so mentally depleted, lay on cots either shivering in fear or so far out of their minds they had permanently checked out on reality. Guards walked the narrow concrete lane carrying shock prods and greedy smiles.

One of the burly, bald headed men who could've passed for a shaved bull greeted Hangman, "Another one for the luxury suite?"

Susan caught sight of what merited a luxury suite. A simple door with pink lettering: *Luxury Suite.*

"Yes, she's a new addition to our collection," Hangman said. "And this one's special. This is Lee Branch's daughter, Susan. She's going to get run through dirty. I want to be the first at her. Nobody touches her. Got that? And if I find out otherwise, everybody on staff right now, including you, Stags, will be executed by me personally."

"No worries, sir," Stags reassured his boss. His eyes showed reverence. "She's all yours. First run."

Hangman opened the nearest cell that was unoccupied. He unhooked Susan's leash from the collar, and forced her by the arm into the cell. Hangman threw the door shut, and hurried off to perform other duties.

Stags stood at her cell door. He was grinding his pelvis into the bars. "I'm going to split you in two when I get the chance. Hangman will open you up, and then I'll be there to really finish you off. I go long and deep."

The guard was panting. Susan noticed his lungs were on the outside of his body. They were covered in mucus that bled through the jailor's dark blue uniform.

"I'll get my turn with you," Stags whispered. "Me and you have a date in the luxury suite. Be thinking about me, sweetie. Know you're on my mind, baby."

Stags dragged the electric prod across the iron bars. Jagged blue forks of electricity shot forth from the prod in all directions. Susan screamed, backing into a corner to avoid any chance of being jolted.

Stags enjoyed his moment, then he returned to his duty of patrolling the cells like nothing had happened.

Susan sat on the greasy cot. She eyed the sink in the wall that was the color of nicotine, and the toilet without a lid. The floor was sticky with dried blood, snot, and semen. Nobody cleaned this place. This was designed to demoralize and degrade. She had been in here mere minutes. What would days do to her? Weeks?

Her neighbors were silent, sitting rigid in their beds. They refused to meet her gaze. If anybody made a sound, she assumed Stags paid them a visit.

There wasn't much for her to do now, but wait and play along. The longer she stayed here, absorbing the stink and the atmosphere of hopelessness, the more Susan craved escape.

Running away wouldn't be enough, Susan realized. The guards, the dinosaurs, the cannibals, and Hangman all spelled trouble. As soon as she stepped foot out of this cell, she would have to kill to protect herself. Susan easily reconciled the notion of murdering in the name of self-defense.

She returned to the simple plan.

Listen for the screaming to start.

Part Three: All Shit Hits the Fan

Streak in the Night

Pierce was neck-deep in dirt. The dinosaur bone served well as a shovel as he pummeled furiously at the soft earth. He had worked below the perimeter fence and was now crossing over to the other side. He realized a few things as his body worked mindlessly at the task of digging. The people in charge hadn't faced off with a worthy opponent before. The cannibals wouldn't understand technology, and how it could be breached. Dinosaurs were in the same predicament. They feared pain, and couldn't think beyond digging under a fence and entering the compound. Now that he was where he needed to be, standing on the opposite side of the fence, Pierce wasn't sure what to do. There was no spotlights or alarms going off. Nobody knew he was here.

What are you going to do now? Knock on the front door and demand them to hand over Susan? She could be dead. You're going to be dead if you don't start thinking.

Until he could prove otherwise, Pierce considered Susan alive.

Pierce sprinted across an open grassy area. It took him minutes to reach the wall of the compound. He spotted watchtowers at a front gate, and nothing else. He scanned the building for windows, doors, or any breachable point. Pierce only noted the front gate, a circular courtyard area, and double doors that led inside. This was where a giant spotlight illuminated the area. They had planned this well. Only one place to enter or leave. That made the guard's job easier. That didn't leave much for Pierce to do.

His mind turned over the possibilities. Every avenue started and ended with those front double doors. He had to find safe access through those doors. Then he could comb the inside rooms and learn the layout.

This plan is outright fucked.

Pierce imagined the mercenaries chiming in, berating him that he indeed was fucked, and fucked hard.

No, I'm not fucked. I made it this far against the odds. I'll keep going. If I can't find Susan, I'll take this place down. I'm not slapping the cuffs on anybody's hands. I'm bringing down the guillotine blade. I'm chopping off heads. I'm going to serve my own brand of jus—

Voices.

Pierce stopped thinking, and stayed crouched down against the wall.

"You mean you told Hangman you murdered that asshole under the waterfall, and you didn't really kill him?"

"He hit me good over the head with something. I'm still cleaning the blood out of my eyes." Pierce recognized Willy's voice. The man was good and pissed off. "I was dizzy walking the whole way here. I called you, buddy, because I don't trust anybody else to help me without ratting me out to the boss."

"You did the right thing, Willy. I'll help you find that bastard."

"I was almost attacked by a Stegosaurus on the way here. The head on that long neck about reached down and swallowed me up whole. I'm telling you those green fuckers got a beef with us. They act scared, but I swear, if they had their chance, they'd kill us all. They want our blood and bones."

"Forget about those dinosaurs," Willy's friend reassured him. "We got this handled. One day, Hangman will get the okay from the big bosses to 86 those prehistoric assholes. Until then, we keep our cool. I bet you the man you're looking for got gobbled up by some wild beast out there. You're probably worrying about a dead guy."

"I don't know. This guy, he's slippery. We shot him out in the ocean, and even with a bullet in him and no supplies, he managed to survive. He can't be an environmentalist. This guy has training. He could be from another organization that can do more than make hemp products and churn out organic foods."

While they were talking, they were both smoking a cigarette and coming right his way. It was dark, Pierce reasoned, but if they kept coming, they would notice him. Pierce scrambled to think. Running would be stupid. The only thing to do was to hold onto the hope that they would somehow overlook him.

"Hey, look over there!"

Damn it all!

Willy was the second pair of eyes to land on Pierce. "Wait a minute. That's the guy. That's him!"

"Great. Let's beat the shit out of him."

Pierce didn't give the speaker a chance to take a single step towards him. He remembered the dinosaur bone he clutched in his hands. Pierce drove it up high, swinging down like a hammer over the henchmen's skull. The bone shattered on impact. Bone to skull, the crippling connection sounded like an exploding cinder block. The man buckled as blood flowed down his face. Landing on the grass, his feet did a nerve dance, and he was either dead, or on his way to being dead.

Willy was a human spear, launching himself at Pierce. They both landed against the bare grass and rolled, rolled, rolled. Willy was all fists and savage anger. Pierce didn't know what hit him. His ribs, skull, jaw, and kidneys swelled from the pain of the swift beat down. Another winning blow from Willy, and Pierce's skull rang like a gong. He realized how weak he was, suffering the impossible survival conditions, and fighting against an enemy that had every advantage.

Willy was hysterical. The madman was hurling curses, unleashing tracks of spit, yanking Pierce's hair, biting his neck and shoulder, and unleashing every ounce of venom from the darkest pit of his soul. Pierce was overpowered by the henchmen. He only had one shot of re-taking control of the fight. Pierce unleashed a growl so animal, so alien, Willy lost his gall. Bunching up his fist, channeling every remaining bit of strength left inside him, the catapult of flesh and bone and force was snapped back, and spring-ejected forward. Pierce's wicked punch landed under Willy's chin. His teeth clacked together, and Willy's eyeball shot out of the socket again, but this time, the pink orb attached snapped. Willy's eyes bounced onto the ground. The orb was quickly lost in the dark.

Willy was howling in horror. Pierce shut him up with a scissor kick to the solar plexus. Willy flew backwards ten feet. Pierce had no idea how far they'd wrestled each other until he noticed the main building was at least thirty yards behind them. Willy crashed through the gate of a fenced in box, and when his body collided against the steel box inside, everything turned into explosions of electricity. Then a great plume of fire rocked the night. Pierce was thrown back by the burst of heat and the concussion of the blast. Willy was flailing in the box, being cooked alive by wild flames and branches of electricity.

Pierce got back up and ran towards the building for cover. Somebody would notice the commotion, and quick.

Luck was on his side. He had kicked Willy into what supplied power to their home base. Pierce saw what few lights from inside the building go dark. Henchmen were pouring out of the front of the building. The way they were reacting, they had never come upon this inconvenience before.

Pierce formed a new plan and executed it.

Call of the Raptor

The velociraptor pawed at the earth, staying low and keeping its senses keen. The dinosaur had seen the man approach the fence with fearlessness. The raptor knew what happened to those who touched the fence. Zap! Instant death. That's why the dinosaur watched with interest as Pierce had dug into the earth with a bone and went underneath the fence to the other side unharmed.

Curious, the raptor approached the hole. The creature watched the man cross to the other side of the fence with interest. Minutes passed, and the raptor stood there in indecision. Fear kept its actions at bay—but only for so long.

The raptor could sense the electrified sound coming off of the fence. The vibrations bragged of doom. The raptor had seen its fellows dare to touch the fence, and come away with scorched skin.

The raptor remained on the outskirts of the crude hole. It sniffed around, pawed at the ground with its razor claws, and remained indecisive.

A great explosion erupted nearby. The raptor turned its head to the side and caught sight of the orange ball of flames. It heard those glorious screams of human pain. Screams of pain meant meat in its mouth and hot blood streaming down its face. The raptor, and its kind, feared the humans because they were the torturers. Through that fear, the raptor still craved the blood of its enemies. This was instinct, pure and carnal.

The raptor's keen senses could hear it—or rather, didn't hear it. The buzz from the fences stopped. The raptor knew something had changed. The risk was worth the downfall, because the raptor craved the fresh blood of its enemies; to gnaw on their bones, to stop their hearts, and to rise up and be at the top of the food chain once again.

The raptor threw its head back and unleashed a piercing call into the night. High pitched, crossed with an eagle and the guttural power of a dragon, the raptor's shriek touched all the ears of the dinosaurs on the island. Every prehistoric beast perked in the jungle.

Dinosaurs pounded through the miles to reach the raptor and heed their wild urges. Every beast ran together, unified in a common cause to devour the humans. The harder they stomped, the more their fear vanished. The dinosaurs were no longer natural enemies. They were a team of bloodthirsty pillars of carnage.

It wouldn't be long before the lone raptor would no longer stand alone outside the fence. When the island's population of dinosaurs arrived, those fences would be going down, and the feast would begin.

Call of the Cannibal

Bones were all that remained of Staff, Lords, and Berkley's bodies. Nothing had gone to waste. The cannibals devoured every scrap of flesh, slab of muscle, ounce of blood, and pound of internal organs. Some of their remains currently simmered in a great pot over the fire. The tribe had eaten well tonight. If it weren't for the occasional human that crossed their paths, they would have to survive on vegetation. They were much like the dinosaurs on this island; they much preferred meat.

A feeling of intense sadness swept over the tribe as they surrounded the great pit of fire to reflect on their day. Meat was getting harder and harder to come by these days. Their dinosaur friends were attacking them more often. "Safe" was a rare feeling on this island.

The tribe heard the raptor's shriek echo off every pocket of the island.

They knew what that sound meant.

Meat, and lots of it!

Strung out, tired of being the weaker of the species, the tribe rose up from their positions around the fire. The cannibals worked fast to gather stone axes and bone hammers, and followed the sound of the raptor's shrieks. The horde of wild savage men and women marched forward, unleashing wild tribal calls, trying to match the much louder calls of the dinosaurs.

The cannibals were fast approaching the perimeter gates.

Dr. Prater's Assessment

Joey stood in line to visit Dr. Prater. His fellow workers waited with him, standing in the cordoned line for however long it took for the doctor to see them. Joey was in line for thirty minutes, but it could've been three hours, and he wouldn't have noticed it. Susan Branch was on his mind, or rather, Mindy Kates.

Mindy was Joey's wife before he was incarcerated for manslaughter. The details of his former life were vague to him after working on the island for so many years, but the one detail that did register: the memory of his wife, sweet Mindy. Susan was a dead ringer for Mindy. Susan had the same pale skin, supple thighs, breast size, striking red hair, and enticing green eyes as Mindy. Susan became Mindy in Joey's mind. Even Joey's second head agreed that Susan was his wife. Hangman had locked her up in the basement of this place, and what horrors his wife would endure down there quickly troubled Joey. He refused to let a man touch her, and yet Joey subserviently stayed in line to see the doctor. Helplessness prevented him from acting out any retaliation.

Saggy-fleshed faces, multiple limbed people, and those with organs pumping life outside their bodies surrounded Joey. Why didn't he march down to the basement and overtake Stags? It was Stags's shift. Joey could overpower the guard. He didn't care if the man was double his size. Joey had two heads now, and he could outthink any enemy.

Joey was sweating nervously just thinking about acting out his plan.

"Joey, Dr. Prater is ready to see you now."

The guard, Bellows, called his name. Joey couldn't overtake Bellows. The man clutched the electric prod in his right hand, and his left hand pointed at the door to Dr. Prater's office. If Joey dared to escape, it would be hundreds of volts of electricity entering his body. Joey had no chance.

Joey said hello to Bellows and played along with the situation. He entered Dr. Prater's office. The odd tang of chemical preservative hit him first. If an outsider would've stepped into this room without any idea what this place was, they wouldn't assume it was a physician's office. They would think this was a mad scientist's study. Glass jars lined the shelves with preserved growths. Hideous cancers were big enough to own small eyes, lungs, and other organs, as if the organs themselves were trying to become their own person. In the larger aquariums, livers, spleens, hearts, and gallbladders swam about the water with tiny makeshift arms, legs, and eyes, and some, even with mouths that tried to talk.

Dr. Prater was placing a tumor with a single eyeball into a jar of fresh preservative. The doctor didn't acknowledge Joey's entrance until Dr. Prater placed that jar on an empty spot on his shelf, and labeled it. When the man turned around, Dr. Prater gave Joey a once over with those astute, scientific eyes. Everything was a specimen to be dissected and conquered to the medical deviant.

The doctor wiped his bloody hands on the front of his lab coat. He was always covered in random smears of blood. Dr. Prater was in his mid-sixties, his hair was a bold white, and his face was haggard with decades of morbid scrutiny.

"I'm going to record our session," Dr. Prater said. He started a tape recorder slathered in countless shades of blood. "Today is very important, Joey. It's time to play with science."

Joey's flesh crawled.

Dr. Prater had been talking about this moment for weeks.

The doctor wanted to sever his second head.

"I know you've enjoyed your friend on your shoulder." A wry laugh snuck out of the doctor. "He's the bug in your ear who gives you the smart things to say to your coworkers when they make fun of you. You've been in more fistfights because of your little friend. But that's not why I want to extract him from your body. I want to see if you'll grow a new head in its place. And if that happens, how many heads will grow out of your body? I love collecting growths from the human body. Imagine how many heads I could collect from your body, Joey.

"This isn't a bad thing, Joey. I know he's your friend. Imagine the next head, Joey. They'll be just as friendly, and who knows, it could be a lady head that pops up next time. The possibilities are copious."

Dr. Prater moved to the corner of the room where his table was located. Steel medical instruments were altered to become greater cutting tools. Scalpels were triple-bladed. Bone saws owned extra sets of jagged teeth. Pinch clamps were designed to dig into the skin like fish hooks. Dr. Prater enjoyed dissection, blood spilling, and recording the sounds his patients made during the process. The doctor was trying to decide which tool to use to cut off Joey's second head.

"Now Joey, you still haven't answered my questions. Does the head think for itself? What does it tell you to do? Can it hear me? If it can, what is it saying to you now?"

Joey's second head spoke in a monotone voice. It had no panic or insistence in its voice.

Tell him you hear nothing.

You only hear your own thoughts.

"I hear nothing," Joey parroted. "Only my own thoughts."

Dr. Prater played his fingers over the blade of a steel cleaver. "That doesn't sound like something you'd say, Joey. I've asked around about you. They say you're reading books now. You never read books before. The closest thing you get to reading is what it says on those sluts' backs when you fuck them. I'm not stupid, Joey. I've done my homework on you. The things you say to your fellow co-workers, they say you're talking like a man who has gone to college. We both know you're not that smart. Frankly, you're dumb as shit. So tell me, what does the head tell you to do? Last chance to fess up before I cut it off. I can keep it alive, Joey; I'll make the head talk, and tell me what I ask. I'll send electrodes through its brain until it speaks. Why won't it talk to me, Joey? *Why*, Joey, *why?*"

Dr. Prater's face was set in a deep scowl. He wiped spittle from the edges of his mouth, and inadvertently smeared blood on his cheek.

I only want the best for you, the head spoke to him in Joey's mind. *They don't care about you, Joey. Who can truly care about you if they're not a part of you? You miss your wife. She's downstairs. We'll save her, and we'll all get off this island. This place is good for no one.*

"It's good for no one," Joey let it slip.

"What was that, Joey? Did the head speak to you? Is that what it said, Joey." Dr. Prater slammed his arms against the table. Dozens of steel instruments clattered to the floor. "Tell me, tell me, tell me! Stop holding back! Nobody holds back anything from me!"

You want to see your wife again, don't you? She'll love you unconditionally. Love knows no restrictions, Joey. Time, distance, mutation...the heart will always understand.

We talked about what to do, Joey.

Now's the time.

"I'll tell you what the head says to me," Joey growled. "You really want to know?"

"Yes," Dr. Prater begged. The man's eyes were wide and anticipating greatness. "Please, Joey. Tell me everything. Don't hold back a word."

"It says you must be stopped!!!"

Joey smashed his arms, elbows, and fists into the nearby aquariums. Dozens of glass tanks were shattered. Tumors, living organs, and oddities from the human body slithered onto the ground. They instantly attacked Dr. Prater, racing up his legs and sinking into his skin as if melting through. Dr. Prater buckled over in pain. Joey didn't stick around to watch what happened next. He stormed out of the door and faced Bellows.

You can take him, Joey. Show him how strong you really are. You're not as weak as they always thought. You're so much stronger than they are. It's time they get a demonstration of your power.

"Joey!" Bellows couldn't believe what he was hearing in Dr. Prater's office. "What did you do to Dr. Prater?"

Joey didn't give Bellows a chance to use that electric prod in his hands. With a force unknown to Joey's experience, he reared back his fist and drove his knuckles into Bellows' face. Every bone caved in from the pressure. Bellows shit his pants. When Joey dislodged his fist, the man's face was no more. Joey shook off brains from his fingers as the guard's corpse toppled to the ground.

Everybody in line stared gaping eyed at Joey.

That's when the power went out.

Joey cut through the room, weaving in the darkness between dumbfounded co-workers, exited the room, and headed right for the emergency stairway.

His wife still needed to be saved.

Breakout

Lee Branch knew his time was limited. Once Susan, a beautiful woman, was thrown into the basement and into that degrading pleasure pad for the island's workers, she'd be raped, defiled, and abused. Lee had little time to save her.

Dr. Prater had injected him with chemicals and pollutants from dozens of corporations. Greens, purples, oranges, reds, and yellows had entered his bloodstream. Globo Corps considered it his punishment for disturbing their affairs. They sure made one hell of a mistake. They went overboard with the contaminants. It had mutated, and turned him into a hideous abomination. This transformation also made him so much stronger and pissed off. He was always raging and ready to take it out on these assholes who ran the show.

Lee played his hands down his exposed belly. All they gave him to wear was a pair of white pants made out of trash bag material. His skin was so melted, he couldn't wear normal clothes. It didn't matter. It wasn't his skin that mattered.

What was inside him did.

The waxen flesh over Lee's abdomen boiled. Lee's navel opened up and out came the long, thick, and so very powerful pink visceral snake. Lee's intestines wound out of his body with such speed and force, it punched through the steel door, and sent the barrier spinning into the guard who happened to be walking in front of it. The guard's face was a bloody mess, and his eyeballs were dancing in his head. Lee didn't give the bastard a chance to pick up his electric prod or recover. The end of his intestine, a circular mouthed suction hole, wrapped around the guard's head, sucked it off of his neck with a hundred bone breaking sounds, and then spit it out across the hallway. Those imprisoned in the cells cheered and hollered.

Lee's intestines coiled back into his belly. The pink circular mouth stayed three inches out of his navel, poised to strike like a viper when a threat posed itself.

He rushed to the main control panel. Lee was confused when the guards who normally stayed at the main station were missing. Something was happening elsewhere in the facility, and he could hear noises echo through the walls. The sounds were coming from outside.

Lee grabbed the keys to the cell doors, and began unlocking the environmentalists from the rooms and torture chambers. Many were also affected by chemical exposure. Faces were melting, bodies were pulsating with cancers and tumors, but right now, they no longer cared. They saw Lee, and they knew they were saved. Fifty people were in the hallways now preparing to take on their captors, when the area went dark.

Now Lee really knew something was going down.

He kept freeing the prisoners the best he could without the lights on.

Once he was finished, he navigated his way in the dark to locate the stairs leading to the basement level.

Susan was still very much in danger.

Hangman's Plan

The workers on the island had grown lazy in their positions of power. What was happening rocked them out of their comfort zones. Hangman realized this as he watched the security camera feed of the man who had smashed Loomis over the head with a dinosaur bone, and tossed Willy into their main power supply. After watching a nice electricity and fire show, everybody was on edge. The base was on limited auxiliary power. Hangman knew full power couldn't be restored until a crew from outside the island arrived to repair it.

This day would come eventually, Hangman thought, standing over the console of security screens and watching things unfold. He viewed numerous security feeds. On one feed, Dr. Prater was writhing on the floor. His specimens latched onto his body, and were eating him alive. Another feed, Joey was overtaking Bellows. Then the goon was racing down the stairs to the basement floor. In a more interesting feed, Lee Branch was freeing the environmentalist prisoners from their cells.

Hangman had lost track of the man who had killed his two workers outside.

The bastard was slippery.

The real problem was fast approaching from outside the gates.

A breach in the fence, no doubt from the human intruder, caught the interest of a single raptor. Now cameras a mile out from the base caught sight of what had to be every dinosaur on the island. The dinosaur front was about to storm the gates. Those gates had no juice. The dinosaurs would smash through the barriers, and take them on.

Why not add another problem, Hangman thought, to the already deep shit dilemma? From the opposite side of the island, the cannibals were coming at them with crude weapons in hand. Somehow, they knew the gates were down too. Call it nature's way of hitting the reset button, or perhaps Karma, or shit luck. Either way, they were about to have a serious war on their hands.

Hangman phoned in to his superior at Globo Corps. The superior didn't have a name. The people behind the curtain were shrouded in secrecy. Hangman told the voice on the other end of the line about the current escalating situation, and asked if they had any ideas for swift courses of action.

"*Preserve the dumping facility. Kill every last enemy on the island, including all native life. Do so at any cost.*"

The caller hung up.

Hangman smiled underneath his red silk kerchief. *Kill every last enemy on the island.* It's what they should've done from the start instead of doing all of this hard work security bullshit. Why they kept the cannibals and dinosaurs alive so long was beyond him. The company might've believed the native life was worth a level of future monetary gain. Now that was up in smoke. I guess Globo Corps was cutting their losses.

Hangman wasn't sure who would survive the night.

He was prepared to see blood shed on both sides.

Whose blood would flow in vain, and whose in victory?

Hangman hit the intercom button and addressed the entire building. "*Workers report to the armory. We've got a situation on our hands. Every dinosaur, cannibal, and prisoner must die tonight. Move fast. We've got little time. The enemy is knocking on our door.*"

The workers abandoned the security checkpoint room, and Hangman rushed the stairs. The armory was on the main floor; every worker on the island crowded the stairway. He enjoyed the expressions of dismay on their faces.

This was going to be one hell of a night.

Hangman opened the stairway door that lead to the main level. He crossed two hallways, pushing through hordes of workers who were forming a line outside the armory's door. Hangman parted the sea of bodies, and hit the code to unlock the keypad's door. When he opened it, Hangman gave a short speech before letting his workers have their chance to pick their weapons.

"We've got a prison breakout in progress. Dinosaurs are seconds from battering down our doors. Cannibals are right behind them ready to eat the flesh from our backs. I want every enemy slaughtered. No prisoners. We're cleaning the slate. Use any means necessary. Work together to vanquish this threat. No rules. Only kill them all. And I want you to enjoy it. I WANT YOU TO FUCKING GET OFF ON IT! Use their blood as lubrication to jerk off. I don't care. Show them no mercy. Show them the insanity inside you.

"Grab the weapons you deem most worthy to the cause, and make sure you're proficient in their use before picking it up and getting yourself killed. Use what you take. Our superiors have left us a huge selection of items. Survive the night, and I promise you high rewards. Our company is not shy about awarding those who prove worthy to the cause. You've sacrificed so much, why let this threat steal our achievements here on the island?

"Now go out there, and finish 'em off! Bathe in their blood. Dance in death. Rape their bodies. Savage their souls. Spill their blood in the name of victory. Bring so much fear into them, their blood boils at the very sight of you. They might outnumber us, but we've got the firepower to blow their heads out of their ass to goddamn infinity!"

Hangman threw open the armory's door. The crowd of workers stampeded inside. He watched flame throwers ripped from the steel shelves along side M-60's, M-16's, rocket launchers, M79 grenade launchers, grenades by the case-load, Winchester, Mossberg, and Remington shotguns, SPAS-15 machine guns, Gatling guns, modified elephant guns that fired mini heat-seeking rockets, boxes of dynamite, C-4 charges, riot gear, and in the very back, jet packs armed with rocket launchers, and machine guns. Thousands of weapons flew out that door in minutes. Hangman stayed with the group, barking orders, boosting morale, and bringing out the savages in all of them.

"Pussy by the pound to those who survive tonight," Hangman promised. "Top shelf pussy. Hot neon pink pussy. Pussy that folds like origami. The kind of pussy that steps out of your dreams and sits right on your cock. The type of pussy that's never dry. The caliber of pussy that makes you bark like a dog. No questions asked, you want it, you got it, and if we can't find it, it doesn't fucking exist. If you can't think of the kind of shit you're into, then talk to me, and I'll help you. I'll show you everything that has a hole you can fuck. Bottom line, you're getting off!

"Many of you have killed on a regular basis. Now I'm giving you bigger and better tools to provide the means of true slaughter. Don't let me down. If you're still standing by the end of the night, we shall party like GODS!"

Hangman and his battle-ready crew bolted out the front doors of the compound, and met the threat lurking in the near distance.

War was about to commence.

The Search Continues

Pierce had very little time to orchestrate his plan after Willy's body was cooked crispy. He stole the other dead guard's outfit, put it on, and was headed towards the front entrance when hundreds of guards stormed out the front doors. Pierce thought for a second they were after him. He was about run like hell in the opposite direction, when he heard things coming closer beyond the perimeter gates.

His spine stiffened at the sound of the singing cannibals unleashing their war cries. Worse yet, the sonic boom stomping of something very large and pissed off. A literal stampede of dinosaurs were charging for the base. He could see their shapes become clearer through the thick of the jungle. Elongated necks could see well over the treetops, while other threats remained in the shadows of the jungle. Any minute, the packs of dinosaurs and cannibals would storm the place.

Pierce kept changing his plan. He only had one mission, and that didn't involve going head-to-head with cannibals, dinosaurs, or mutated men. Susan and Lee Branch could be in that building somewhere. He owed it to them to search out the building, locate them, and form a plan from there to get off this island without anybody getting killed.

Pierce clung to the shadows as he approached the building's entrance. He heard orders being barked from a single man as the henchmen took position on the open grass ready to intercept the incoming threat. Pierce was happy to have his back to the incoming battle.

The foyer beyond the entrance featured the mounted human heads of environmentalists.

What has been going on here?

This is truly sick.

Pierce had to learn the layout of the building. Most of the hallways were darkened. At each corner, emergency lights bathed the way in yellowish beams. Each hallway appeared to be the same: closed doors leading to offices, laboratories, and secret rooms.

Pierce tried the elevator.

It didn't work.

Damn it.

Where do I go?

This rescue mission is fucked.

In two seconds, the rescue mission no longer mattered. He heard the scrape of razor claws against the linoleum. The scrapes were spread out and soft, the sound of a predator tracking its prey. Pierce could turn his back, find out what was stalking him, and run for his life, but if he did that, he would burn that single moment to escape. There was no doubt what was behind him. Something covered in scales, armed with sharp as steel teeth, and very, very eager to take a chunk out of his ass.

Pierce bolted for the emergency stairs door. The predator gave a hiss, and bolted after him. Lucky for Pierce, the raptor was much farther down the hallway than he previously imagined. That bought him just enough time to force open the door, throw himself across the threshold, and slam the door closed.

The barrier was useless.

The raptor punched it right off the hinges. Pierce and the door were thrown down half a flight of stairs, and he scrambled to collect himself. Adrenaline was on his side, and he was able to think fast enough to be a worthy opponent in the fight. Pierce grabbed the door with both arms, and used it as a shield.

Nails against chalkboard was all he could hear as the raptor unleashed piercing howl after piercing howl, and slashed at the steel. A literal shower of sparks sprayed everywhere. Through the tiny window in the door, Pierce could see gnashing teeth, and the glowing black eye of the hungry raptor. The force of the raptor's punch kept sending Pierce back several steps. He was at the end of the stairway. He was losing the strength in his arms to hold up the door, and his legs were wobbly after absorbing several blows from the deadly enemy. He was at a loss to figure out how to escape this predicament.

Options were severely limited, but Pierce lucked out again. He admitted to himself he was one lucky bastard. Even the dumb had luck, and Pierce had hit the dumb lottery. The luck might've been dumb, Pierce reasoned, but what he would do with his fortune would be high fucking brow.

Three stair steps from his position, someone from the staff had been doing something to the wall that required a sledgehammer. He imagined someone installing a piece of emergency equipment, or a phone box, or God knew what. Pierce didn't care. There it stood, propped against a wall: a sledgehammer.

The raptor reared back its front legs to pound the door again. Pierce rammed the door against the raptor, jumped the three steps, claimed the sledgehammer, and charged back at the prehistoric foe swinging.

Pierce swung at air on the first swing. After the second swing making a disappointing swish sound, Pierce tripped backwards. He barely dodged a slashing set of claws. Rising back to his feet, panting hard, and covered in burning sweat, Pierce knew if he didn't swing that sledgehammer and make it count, he would be dino meat.

Pierce hit the ground on all fours. The raptor had spun around, swinging his tail to pulverize him. The raptor missed. Its tail struck the wall so hard, it smashed through, and became stuck.

"That's it, you green motherfucker! I'm bringing this down on your fucking head!"

Pierce channeled every ounce of determination and rage into one hammer's fall. Direct hit! The sledge landed with enough force to shatter a house's foundation. The raptor's eyes burst out of its sockets, followed by two generous spurts of high-pressured blood.

The raptor folded over on the ground, dead.

Standing there with a sledgehammer dripping red, Pierce collected his breath. He wasn't allowed to collect much of that breath, when a set of hands grabbed him from behind and growled, *"He's one of them. Kill him!"*

First Front

Hangman stayed back from the front line to call in reinforcements. It became incredibly clear men with guns wouldn't be enough to battle the dinosaurs coming their way. He grabbed the radio receiver from the driver's side of the jeep, and instructed all vehicle units to report to the front lines. Hangman had a few surprises for these dinosaurs and cannibals. He could feel the cords of sinew and bone shape a hideous smile underneath his silk scarf.

Hangman was prepared for bloodshed.

His own lust for death had been anointed tonight.

Hangman grabbed his megaphone, and instructed his team. "Wait for my word to fire."

The first set of gates were battered down by a mix of brontosaurus and stegosaurus beasts. All around the perimeter, the barriers were toppled down by hordes of angry dinosaurs. T-Rex's finished off the concrete poles that wouldn't give to the smaller dinosaurs' attempts. The base was breached at every angle.

Hangman decided to change the main formation in front of the base. "Form a tight circle! Cover each other. I want those with jetpacks airborne. Those with grenade launchers, target the larger dinosaurs. Turn those triceratops inside out with machine gunfire.

And don't forget about the cannibals! OPEN FIRE NOW!!! I WANT EVERY ONE OF THEM DEAD!"

Hangman got up out of the jeep's seat, helmed the M-60 gun turret in the back, and started blasting. His firing marked the beginning of thousands and thousands of rounds being unleashed.

Ox-man, owning six arms, had six M-16's blazing fury at a wild pack of raptors. Hangman smiled as the bullets chewed the green from their bodies, and turned them into steaming reptile pulp. Watching those six arms change magazines and reload so fast was a wicked show to watch. What wasn't so wicked was the triangular-backed plated stegosaurus that picked up Ox-man by the neck, and threw him up in the air. Ox-man was impaled on one of the triangular spikes on its back.

"Goddamn it! That's one of my best men!"

Hangman concentrated his machine gun fire on the stegosaurus with the dying Ox-man stuck on its back. The bullets barely scratched the heavy plated exterior. Hangman wanted to see the damn thing die. He ordered Quad and Grenade to aim their rocket launchers at the beast.

Quad and Grenade didn't disappoint. Firing their rocket launchers in unison, they each hit their mark. The stegosaurus erupted into a mega plume of sizzling guts and meat. The head just dissolved like the contents of a shaken can of soda.

Quad and Grenade pumped their fists in the air in victory. Both fists were chopped off by the stone axes of the cannibals. Four cannibals with mouths for genitals and faces looking like gnarled veil meat each gutted and disembodied Quad and Grenade in seconds.

Hangman blasted the cannibals with two hundreds rounds of ammunition. The cannibals hit the ground as bloody slop.

"FUCK YEAH! Taste their meat IN HELL!"

Two dozens jeeps with machine gun turrets and rocket launchers joined in the fight. Six jeeps aimed their rocket launchers at the towering T-Rex who was getting dangerously close to the base. The T-Rex's body was blasted into eight pieces. So much blood erupted from the beast, the crimson wave splashed the wheels of the Hangman's jeep before seeping into the ground.

Men on jet packs were airborne, facing the fifty pterodactyls who screeched their wicked intentions across the night sky. Bursts of orange light flickered from the rapid-fire machine guns. Three of the men were overtaken, the flying dinosaurs chewing the men in half. Hangman growled in frustration as he watched his men crash down to the ground in gnarly pieces.

The threats on the ground were a different a matter. Hangman had spent so many rounds trying to take out the cannibals that his gun went dry. A brachiosaurus was stomping right towards his position. Fifty feet high, one-hundred and twenty thousand pounds heavy, the threat was clear. Hangman was thinking fast in the jeep. He grabbed a ream of grenades, a loaded M-16, extras clips, tore a rag from his shirt, and lit it on fire with his pocket lighter. He shoved that burning cloth into the gas tank, drove the vehicle at sixty miles an hour, and at the last moment before taking on the behemoth, he leapt from the vehicle and rolled away.

BA-BOOM!

The brachiosaurus had both its front legs blown to pieces. It landed on its face. A sharp crick sound followed. Its neck was broken.

Dead dinosaur fuck, Hangman thought.

Hangman dodged a collection of poison darts from the raging cannibals. The wooden darts landed all around him, sticking up from the ground. He was a lucky bastard. Not a single one touched him. If one of those had pierced him, serious poison would enter his bloodstream. He would be vomiting up his guts and shitting blood until he was dead. Men on the island called it "the seizure shits". The cannibals would pay the price for even attempting to take his life.

Pulling the pin on every grenade on his belt, he launched nine at the cannibals. *Boom, boom, boom, boom, boom, boom, boom, boom, boom.* Bodies exploded in mid-air. A hail of bones and a rain of blood splattered the area. Hangman couldn't count the number of fire-scorched pieces.

It wasn't enough.

More cannibals were coming for him.

Hangman emptied clip, after clip, after clip, after clip. Spewing hot M-16 lead, he watched skin tear, pop, and fold to his machine gun's power. Still more cannibals were approaching him. He was out of magazines. Hangman fell back. He pried sawed off shotguns, Uzis, and high-powered hand guns from teeth-mangled bodies and severed limbs. He fired wildly, trying to find a place to collect himself, and assess the battle zone.

Six pterodactyls picked up a jeep, carried it up high, and dropped it down with a thunderous explosion. Hangman dodged a spinning jeep bumper and a burning human spine simultaneously. A T-Rex was chewing up a jeep in its mouth when the gas tank exploded. T-Rex's head was set ablaze. The behemoth kept chomping down on metal and steel until its skin was downgraded to bone. Once its eyes melted in its head, the T-Rex tower finally toppled over dead.

Binge, a watchtower worker, had a double sized mouth, and was devouring the cannibals, when three arrows pierced his throat. He doubled over in the throws of death, vomiting up his guts, and experiencing the seizure shits.

Seeker, a night security goon, shoved a double-barreled shotgun into the mouth of a bagaceratops. The dinosaur was the size of a medium dog. The whole body went up in a ball of blood. The crazy son-of-a-bitch didn't see the stegosaurus behind him swing its tail. Seeker was lashed by pure force, and the blow cut him in half. Seeker was only a pair of standing legs until a raptor took off with them.

Patch, Robin, Decker, and Scratch were gored on the horn of a triceratops. When the triceratops shook them off, the force was so powerful their bones shattered.

From the air, pieces of jet packs and mutilated remains kept crashing down. Hangman watched in morbid fascination at the legless jetpack man whose guts dangled like fat rope out his pulverized pelvis land in a ball of fire.

Hangman couldn't lie to himself, this was a disappointing show of force. He was naive to trust in men who didn't know real combat. These weren't soldiers; they were fallible men without real guts, balls, or spine.

Let them die in shame, Hangman kept thinking. Let them be shit out of a dinosaur's ass, and returned to the earth to be long forgotten.

Hangman sprinted behind the nearest jeep with these thoughts burdening him. He returned to the focus of battle and survival. A pair of raptors were munching down on Compass's neck to the point he was decapitated. Compass was another treasured member of his staff. There were no good men left.

Staying out of sight, Hangman crawled on the ground to hide underneath a mangled pile of half and quarter bodies. He quickly decided against that plan when he spotted the cannibal children noshing down on toes, playing tug-of-war with intestines, and sticking their fists into the wide-open maws of decapitated heads. He crawled elsewhere, trying to find a safe spot, and failing.

Teams of cannibals were feasting on the remains of both dead workers and fallen dinosaurs. The sound of reptile and cannibal feasting sickened his stomach, not in disgust, but in shame.

Damn them all!

This wasn't a battle.

This was a slaughter.

One man had caused this mess. The son-of-a-bitch who dug underneath the fence and drew the dinosaurs and cannibals to the base. One man had deconstructed a well-oiled machine in less than a few hours. Hangman swore he would find that bastard, and show him the meaning of agony. First, Hangman had to do the work of many men by himself.

Hangman stood up proudly on the decimated battlefield.

He removed the silk scarf around his mouth and tossed it aside.

Now it's killing time.

The New Front

"He's one of them! Kill him!"

Pierce was tackled by dozens of people. When he hit the ground, he was kicked and beaten by the angry group. Pierce was gripped by pain. He tried to beg them to stop, but he couldn't say a word. He was drowning in a sea of violence. Pierce could see his aggressors; many of them were mutated. Pierce noticed a woman with hands at her breasts. Another man had bone daggers sticking out of the tips of his fingers. Most of them had melted flesh that had hardened into bizarre expressions. They were waxberry candle people.

Everybody wasn't mutated. The others were women adorned in tatters for clothing. They were dirty, downtrodden, and angry as hell. Pierce tried again to identify himself not as the opposition. He wanted to tell them that he had to steal a worker's clothes so he could get into the base undetected. Pierce tried to say all of this, and only got out the words, "I'm looking for Susan Branch!"

A bold, authoritative voice shouted over the rage of the crowd. "Everybody stop! Hold on! I know him! He's on our side."

The beating didn't stop.

"I said he's on our side! Stop what you're doing, and listen to me!"

No good.

The crowd was incensed to the point of craving violence.

Something reached around his midsection and coiled its middle multiple times. Pierce was lifted up over the crowd's head. Everybody stopped and gasped. Pierce dangled over their heads well out of reach of their fists.

"It's you!" Pierce heard a woman's voice speak. "I thought you were dead! Put him down, Dad. It's Pierce Range. He's on our side."

Pierce couldn't believe what was holding him up in the air.

Lee Branch's intestines!

Pierce was placed back on the stairway. The mob backed off, and Lee Branch approached him. Lee was barely recognizable. The man wore white plastic pants, and the rest of him was that melted waxberry texture. A section of pink intestine stuck out of his belly button. Pierce wasn't sure what to say to the man in this strange situation. Lucky for Pierce, Susan stepped between them to end the awkward moment.

Susan explained to her father how she happened to run into Pierce in Florida, and how he helped them get to the island. Pierce felt the pain of the bullet where it entered and exited his body. Pierce apologized for not being able to save Susan from being captured. He apologized for everything.

Lee was understanding. "Nothing could've prepared anybody for what's on this island, and I lost good men on this mission. I should've done my homework before coming here. Globo Corps tricked us, but now's the time we rise up against them. We're re-taking this island. It's going to be easy."

"Easy, huh? How so?" Pierce scoffed. "They have so many men out there. There's only so many of us. We don't stand a chance."

"You said it, Pierce," Lee said. "They have so many men *out there*. Listen to them suffer. The dinosaurs and cannibals are taking down their numbers. When the battle calms down, we bust out of here, and kill the rest of them. They've tortured and mutated us. It's time they pay for that. The Green Project isn't over, this is only the beginning. We are the new front!"

The captives, the mutated, and a few of the island's workers who'd flipped sides, vocalized their approval. They cheered, and spoke words of encouragement.

The moment was broken up by the sound of a wall shattering. That's exactly what it was, Pierce deduced. Things were battering against the building with startling force. It sounded like wrecking balls pummeling through concrete.

Everybody's moment of rebellion suddenly downgraded into cowardice. Lee sensed the change in the crowd too. "Everybody topside. We can't stay at the bottom level. It sounds like the dinosaurs have cleaned up Globo Corps's goons. Up the stairs, come on!"

Pierce followed the tide of the fast moving crowd. Parts of the building were caving in; the structure was weakening as more powerful blows threatened to decimate the base. Up one flight of stairs, they reached the top floor in a hurry.

Once they were on the main floor, everybody was running towards the foyer with the mounted heads on the wall. The only problem, there was no more foyer! Hordes of dinosaurs were bashing their bodies and skulls to destroy everything. They hallway was exposed at both angles to the open air.

Pierce searched for Susan and Lee. He wanted to help bring them to safety, but Lee was missing. Susan was grabbed from behind by a two-headed goon. Pierce heard a part of what the goon was saying as he dragged Susan out into the night.

"*Mindy, it's me. It's Joey. I love you. I'll keep you safe. I'll...*"

Everybody from the basement level scattered. Pierce realized he stood alone in the hallway. Things were happening so fast that Pierce's senses couldn't keep up. What did compute were the dozen raptors coming in at him from one end of the hallway. At the other end, a giant T-Rex head peeked into the hallway, and targeted Pierce. The T-Rex raged, sending up its monstrous reptile call for death. It pummeled through what was left of the wall, and bashed through it easily.

Pierce had no place to go.

He would be dead in seconds.

Mad Doctor

Dr. Prater wasn't dead. His specimens had failed to murder him in his office. Far from it. They improved him. He was more alive now than he ever was in that healthy body. He studied disease, and was obsessed with mutations all of his life. Show him tumors that bled every color of pus. All the colors of the puss wheel! Bring on the cancer. Show him the human body and its sickness. Dr. Prater wanted to experience it all, firsthand.

The doctor was a pillar of walking, dripping, seeping, oozing malady. The disease machine was ready to inject everything with his sickness so he could dissect it, study it, even fornicate with it. His brain swelled with polyps and nasty disgusting cancers unknown to previous science. Dr. Prater was a living Petri dish.

One thing kept repeating in his mind.

Joey's second head.

He wanted that head on a slab. Dr. Prater wanted to grow hundreds of the heads. He would make each head talk to him. Joey's body was a head machine, and Dr. Prater wanted that machine to produce.

Dr. Prater would have his fucking heads.

All he had to do was find Joey.

Dr. Prater stalked the outside of the base. He had seen the group rise up from the basement, and run right into the killing field. Joey would be out there somewhere.

I will have Joey's head.

A million heads for me!

A triceratops charged at Dr. Prater, and he held out both hands. His hands folded down at the wrists as if on a hinge. This exposed the veins inside his arms. The veins sprayed sizzling hot green sickness; the high-pressure spurts covered fifteen yards. The triceratops's face instantly melted. Boils and tumors rose up along its body, and grew so big they popped. The pops were like grenades. All that was left of the beast was a boiling green puddle.

More dinosaurs were after him. Raptors from the left, another T-Rex right in front of him, and a pterodactyl was lowering to scoop him up and feast upon him.

The T-Rex got him first. Lowering its head, the T-Rex swallowed Dr. Prater whole. Down the powerful throat, Dr. Prater's body secreted acid from every pore. The throat dissolved all around him. The T-Rex couldn't breathe. Dying, it tumbled forward, and choked on the acid rushing down its throat. When the T-Rex hit the earth, Dr. Prater fell free from the hole in the dinosaur's throat.

Recovering himself, Dr. Prater plucked a tumor from his belly, and pitched it at the cannibal warrior wanting to attack him. It stuck to the cannibal's face, and ate into his features. The tumor turned into two, and two metamorphosed into eight, and eight into fifty, and fifty into hundreds. Thirty seconds later, the cannibal's entire body was being eaten alive by tumors with teeth.

Nothing could hurt the mad doctor.

Dr. Prater plucked boils, growths, and bodily anomalies from his anatomy, and used them as defense.

He kept searching for Joey, and that precious head.

After dispatching a brontosaurus by raking his nails across its reptilian body and injecting a turbo form of the black plague into its body, Dr. Prater caught sight of Joey.

Joey was firing a machine gun, and protecting a screaming woman from a group of hungry cannibals.

I will have your head, Joey.

Thousands of heads for me!

But first, that woman with Joey must die.

It Takes Guts

Lee was searching for Susan. He lost his daughter in the crowd. Where had she gone? He prayed nothing had killed her. And who was that son-of-a-bitch who kept calling Susan his wife? The madman was delusional—and he had two heads!

Lee had little time to think it over. He scanned the war zone for Susan, while his intestines fought back against the enemies surrounding him. A goon was soaring on a jet pack up high. The goon aimed his machine guns at Lee, but Lee didn't give him a chance. His intestine snaked out of his belly, reached up fifty feet, and ripped off the bastard's left leg. The leg stump gushed blood, and down went the gunner.

Lee dodged a swinging stone axe. A cannibal drenched in blood was coming at him with rage and hunger playing on his face. Lee's intestine punched a hole through the cannibal's belly, and like a bullet, the cannibal's insides fired out his backside.

Surrounded by threats, Lee ripped off a pterodactyl's head, strangled another cannibal, wrapped his guts around an abandoned Jeep, and hurled it at a group of charging brontosauruses.

These actions bought him time. It wouldn't do him any good if Susan was already dead. How could he go on with the blood of his daughter on his hands? He had pushed her into the extreme environmentalist gig at an early age. He was responsible for her safety, and her death would be on him.

Everything went out the window in two seconds.

Lee's sworn enemy appeared between flaming piles of wrecked vehicles and burning bodies. The man who had injected chemicals into his body and got off on the mutations that turned Lee's body into flesh cheese. There stood the orchestrator of everything evil on this island. Hangman noticed Lee from across the battlefield. Hangman indicated with a finger to bring it on.

I won't stop fighting until one of us is dead.

Lee snarled, unleashed a battle cry, and charged at the bastard.

Only One Way Out

Pierce knew his chances at surviving were dwindling the longer he stood in place like an idiot. He searched for an outlet to run. Every broken down wall revealed dinosaurs lurking. He wasn't safe in any direction he chose; this was the end of his life. Maybe he should've taken that walk into the ocean. The cold kiss of water was better than the hot breath of a raptor plunging its mouth into his neck, and eating him alive.

You never were going to take that walk into the ocean. You would've become one of those bums who beg change, and drink themselves to death. You were going to die a sad death. At least you're here fighting for something. Stand tall.

Pierce searched for any other means of survival. There it was, shining like a beacon. Under a pile of broken bricks, Pierce made out the shape of a jet pack. He strapped the device on. It was very heavy, and he struggled to lug it over his shoulders. The dinosaurs were headed right for him. He hurried for the sake of his life.

Pierce pressed a red button. The engine started right up. He was off the ground, and headed straight up with increasing speed. Raptors leapt up, and missed his feet by mere inches. Flying higher, he traveled through the hole in the ceilings, and was outside in the open air. He had a perfect view of the battlefield. What he saw was active devastation. Piles of torn up bodies, dinosaur and human, were scattered between piles of burning wreckage. Whatever battle happened, it didn't last long. Both sides were equally equipped for the kill.

Pierce started taking aim, and picking off what enemies he could. He tried to save who he could from incoming cannibals and dinosaurs. Then Pierce spotted Susan, and she was in serious trouble. He only had seconds left to save Susan before something terrible happened to her. Pierce came up with a plan, and did his best to follow through with it.

The Nasty Doctor

Susan couldn't could slip the hold of the man who kept telling her she was his wife. She remembered Joey from when Hangman gave her a tour of the base. The second head's eye stayed glue to Susan, while Joey was focusing on the man in heavily soiled medical scrubs covered in neon greens, yellows, reds, and browns. The doctor was a walking boil factory. Active sores, lesions, and tumors throbbed and oozed.

"I want that head!" Dr. Prater demanded. "Give me your head, and I'll let you live, Joey."

Joey was pissed. "You're not touching me ever again. Stay back, and I'll let *you* live."

Susan screamed when Dr. Prater raised up both hands. The hands themselves fell down, and stayed attached to the arms like they were on a flesh hinge. Out came spurting green and black juices, and Joey had to throw Susan aside to avoid the flying acid. The acid landed on the dead corpse of a cannibal, and that corpse instantly evaporated.

Susan was free, but she had nowhere to go. She hid underneath the blackened shell of a jeep, and watched the fight unfold between Joey and Dr. Prater.

* * *

Dr. Prater licked the pus dribbling from his polyp-fleshed lips. He dug into his belt and lifted the surgical cleaver. He craved Joey's second head. Just thinking about the cleaver sawing through the meat of the neck caused tumors and cancers to be born along his body, and throb in pure anticipation. The doctor imagined slicing off the head, and another one immediately growing in its place, and slicing that one, and another growing, slicing, and another, slicing, and another, slicing, and another, and another...

Joey stood there, unsure of his next move. Mindy was safe under the jeep for the moment. No harm would come to his wife as long as he had a pulse. What to do with Dr. Prater bogged him down. The doctor clutched onto a cleaver, while Joey was unarmed. Could he overpower the doctor with only sheer force?

He didn't have a chance to make any attempt.

Dr. Prater was fast. He closed in the distance between them. Joey could only follow the fast moving glint of the blade as it arced, and swished through the air. The cleaver was lodged into Joey's chest. Joey fell to his knees; the pain was paralyzing.

He could only look into Dr. Prater's eyes. Those bulbous psychotic orbs beheld only one thing. Joey's second head.

"It's mine! MINE! MINE! MINE!"

Joey wept. He wouldn't escape the island with his wife. His life story ended here on his knees bleeding out.

Joey's second head spoke to him.

I thought we could survive this island. Sorry, kid. That woman wasn't your wife, Joey. I'm sorry I lied to you. You needed to believe in something if we were going to escape together.

Who was I kidding? There's no life for a man with two heads in the real world.

I'm so sorry I lied to you, Joey.

There's only one thing I can do to make it up to you.

Something changed in Joey's eyes; he couldn't see what was happening around him anymore. Mindy sprang into his mind's eye. The silk negligee she wore on their honeymoon. The first time they slept together in their father's truck. The way Joey loved it when she cupped his ass with her hands when they slept together every night. Only sweet memories of the woman he loved played out as the spurts of blood left his body, and he died...

Dr. Prater removed the cleaver. He could hear bone and meat shift within Joey's body upon the extraction. Dr. Prater clutched the red dripping cleaver, and raised it up high to hack through that beautiful head.

"My head, at last!"

The doctor was thrown from revelation to terror.

"*Whaaaaaaaaaaaat?*"

Joey's hands grabbed Dr. Prater's body, and drew him in close. The second head opened it maw, and chomped down on the doctor's neck. What spurted from the doctor's torn jugular burned right through Joey and the head's body.

Dr. Prater fell backwards, choking on the rainbow colors spewing from his neck.

The last thing the doctor computed was a T-Rex crushing him under its foot.

Hungry for Her Flesh

Susan watched the doctor and Joey kill each other. She wasn't sure how she felt about the shocking show of death, nor was she given the time. Arms were reaching for her under the jeep. The jeep itself was being jostled; somebody was trying to turn over the jeep. The cannibals cheered, desiring her warm flesh. She had no way to protect herself. They would reach for her, and strip her of everything worth eating.

Susan dodged bloodied hands clutching at her limbs. They would drag her out and devour her alive. She knew she couldn't keep this up much longer, there was just too many of them.

"Leave me alone! Why are you doing this? I've done nothing to you!"

Susan was out of options besides screaming, when her hand touched a Beretta handgun. She opened fire at the hands reaching for her face. Those bodies quickly backed up in retreat. This was her chance, Susan thought. She crawled out from under the jeep, and sprinted.

The cannibals were right after her.

Susan didn't make it far before something grabbed her from behind.

All she could do was scream.

Jet Pack Attack

The button on the left armrest indicated machine gun turrets. The right armrest controlled the rockets. Pierce learned this quickly. Goons were pursuing him with their mad machine guns barking bullets, and they were hovering at both sides of him. Pierce dropped down low, and watched the bullet crossfire turn into friendly fire as four of the goons blasted themselves. Pierce realized they were so desperate and bloodthirsty, they weren't thinking straight.

Pierce flew back up high, and played a game of chicken with the last goon with a jetpack. He was speeding right at the gunner. Pierce didn't flinch, he only picked up speed. Faster, faster, Pierce was a human torpedo about to smash himself into the target. The goon was alarmed when he realized Pierce wasn't going to flinch. Alarmed, taken by total surprise, the goon fumbled with his controls to avoid Pierce. The goon accidentally dropped so low a T-Rex swallowed him whole. The resulting explosion caused the T-Rex's face to burst into fire and blood spatter.

After the explosion, Pierce heard Susan's screams. Cannibals were reaching under the vehicle, while others were attempting to tip it over. Several gunshots later, Susan crawled out from under the jeep, and ran for her life. Cannibals were chasing her. The poor woman didn't stand a chance; they would catch up to her in seconds.

Time to send them a bullet telegram.

Spewing four hundred rounds, the horde of cannibals were reduced to flailing, bleeding, twitching, tattered bodies. Dinosaurs swarmed the cannibals. Pierce showed the cannibals mercy, and unleashed two rockets. He drilled them home, watching the feasting dinosaurs be turned inside out.

Pierce noticed there weren't any more dinosaurs or cannibals. He scanned the area over and over again. Susan was standing behind a jeep missing its driver, while clutching her gun. Pierce touched down next to her.

"It's going to be okay," Pierce said. "They're all dead. We survived."

Susan's face showed zero relief.

This was far from over.

Pierce watched Hangman in horror. Hangman removed the piece of silk covering his face. The man had no lower jaw, it was all pink exposed muscle tissue. The man's tongue was fat, and could coil and uncoil to great lengths. Pierce cried out when the tongue lashed in his direction. The tongue stuck to his jet pack from fifteen yards away. The pack was ripped from his back, thrown into a pile of burning bodies, and rendered useless.

The tongue coiled back into Hangman's mouth. Pierce imagined a frog's tongue, but this tongue was a hundred times stronger.

Pierce had Susan by the arm. "Get moving!"

They were sprinting in the opposite direction, when the tongue gripped onto a jeep, and threw the vehicle right at them. Together, they dove to avoid the vehicle that flipped in mid-air five times.

A hail of broken up jeeps and dinosaur body parts rained down, trying to crush them. Hangman laughed diabolically between things thrown.

"This island is mine! Nobody leaves alive."

"That's where you're wrong, pal."

Pierce and Susan stopped when they heard Lee's angry voice.

"It's the pizza man," Hangman taunted Lee. "I want my pizza with extra cheese, you pizza faced motherfucker."

Hangman was fast to the draw. The man lashed his tongue, wrapping the pink weapon around Lee's neck, and Pierce thought the man was a goner. Susan gasped. "No, Dad!"

Lee was much faster than Hangman. His long intestine was tight around Hangman's neck. They both had each other's number. Who would be the one to act first? Whose ticket would get punched before the other? This wasn't like a shootout, both of them were destined to die. Judging by Lee's face, he was prepared for death.

Lee spoke to Susan. "Carry on with The Green Project. I love you, Susan. I can die a happy man knowing this son-of-bitch won't occupy this world with you. Goodbye, honey."

Pierce wanted to intervene.

Lee had made his choice.

So had Hangman.

Pierce and Susan stood in mortal shock as intestine and tongue decapitated each other.

Toxic Resurrection

Pierce had nothing to add to the deep silence that quickly set in post-battle. Susan was still staring at her father's dead body, she didn't want to believe he was dead. Hard emotions spliced her face. Pierce could only hold her close, and let her cry. That was all that was left to do for her. Release everything. It would take years to get over such a trauma.

Pierce imagined how they'd have to find their way back home. They could locate the materials to build a raft, or if they located a radio, they could call out to someone. Whatever option was available, they had a lot of work ahead of them. Survival was a gift they would have to earn.

"Come on, Susan. We need to get moving. I'm sure you want off this island as much as I do."

She agreed by nodding her head. Susan was still crying.

Pierce understood.

There was some things you couldn't erase from your mind no matter how hard you tried, Pierce learned tonight. His belief system for the unbelievable had forever changed. The meaning of insane had changed from a short definition to a drawn out dissertation. There was still another page to that dissertation Pierce had yet to mentally write.

The fires were starting to die down. It wouldn't be long before the dark of the night would be reinstated. That's why it was so easy to see the neon green circle several yards ahead of them.

"What is that?" Pierce said, drawn to the neon spot. "It looks so strange. You see it?"

"Don't get too close," Susan warned, wiping the tears from her eyes with both hands. "This island's a cesspool of contamination. God only knows what it is."

Pierce made out the T-Rex leg. It had been crudely torn from its body; the dangling rags of meat on the stump indicated as much.

So how could the damn leg twitch?

Pierce's eyes moved faster to make sense of the horrible sight. The neon green wasn't a circle of color, it was part of a dead body, or so it appeared to be dead. The body was smashed, and lodged into the T-Rex's foot.

He made out a doctor's lab coat, part of a sternum, a smashed neck, and a head with a twitching mouth. That mouth spoke!

"Science has brought me back to life! I am Dr. Prater, and I can't be stopped!"

The rags of meat on the T-Rex leg started bleeding green fluids. Tumors, cancers, and sizzling polyps formed on the leg instantly. The dangling rags of meat reached out for dinosaur heads, cannibal organs, and even junked parts of the jeeps.

"Oh my God!" Susan cried.

Pierce had her by the arm. "Run! Fucking run!"

The monstrosity, glowing neon green and boiling with diseases, rose up from the ground in the shape of a crude dinosaur half the size of T-Rex. The human head, lodged in a mess of squashed organs and steel, laughed at their horror.

"My work will continue. I'm going to put you two under the knife. I'll inject you with every disease so you'll grow things I can cut up and put under a microscope. Your bodies are all mine!"

Pierce couldn't shake the image of the cackling man's face in the middle of the inside out crude collage of human, dinosaur, and Jeep.

They dashed for the jungle. Pierce knew they couldn't stay out in the open. He failed to protect Susan on the way to the island; he wouldn't fail when it came time to getting the fuck off the island.

Holding onto her, pushing her forward, forcing himself to keep up a fast pace, they forged deeper into the jungle. Where could they seek cover? Nowhere, Pierce thought. There wasn't a door solid enough to keep out this beast.

The monster smelled terrible. Pierce imagined meat dipped in shit, marinated in garbage, and baked in a casserole of sunbaked carcass and scorched metal. Pierce could hear the neon fluids drip off its body in a steady downpour. It was like sweat to the freak monster.

"Keep moving! Don't stop for anything!"

Susan had no problem following those simple instructions. Ducking, dodging, weaving, leaping, and sprinting through the dense jungle, they were almost at the opposite end of the island. The ocean was visible, and they would be on the shore in minutes. Pierce had no idea what to do next. How long could they run before they couldn't? They weren't in good shape to keep up the retreat for long. The monster wasn't even winded. It would keep pursuing them until they were dead.

Pierce imagined running up the shore to buy them more time. He was about to tell Susan what to do, when they both had to hit the ground in a hurry.

It's Now Their Island

"*Noooooooooooooooooo!*"

Dr. Prater's screech of intense pain echoed across the entire island. The dawn sun was peeking out over the horizon. Pierce and Susan could see them coming clearly. Thousands of flies the size of softballs swarmed around the stinking waft of dinosaur and human bodies. The collection was a moving black blanket of infernal buzzing. The flies pierced through the soft flesh, and carried bits and pieces away. Splashes of blood was the only thing left of the super monstrosity.

The flies were gone. They could hear their distant buzzing recede until everything returned to silence.

Susan was in shambles. She was stiff to the touch. The poor woman was petrified by fear.

Pierce said what he could up against the unbelievable. "We're getting off this island before God knows what else comes out of the woodwork."

Pierce guided the troubled Susan along the rocks of the shore. He wasn't sure how to get the hell off of the island. The thick fog surrounding the island made it hard to see too far out. He was about to lose himself to frustration when he remembered something.

"I have an idea."

He guided Susan onwards with more energy, even though his body was a wreck. It was amazing to think out of everybody on this island, only two people had survived the night.

Pierce spotted the remains of Susan's boat. He went from one high to another extreme low. The boat was smashed on the bottom, and currently half submerged in water. They wouldn't be taking the boat anywhere.

Susan seemed to recover, and sprinted to the boat.

"Wait, where are you going?"

"Follow me, Pierce. Trust me."

They treaded the rocks carefully, and reached the boat. Susan was stepping on the deck that threatened to break into pieces at any moment. She reached into the back, opened a compartment, and ripped back on a cord. With a rush of air, a large orange floatation device blew itself up.

"Thank God the float wasn't damaged," Susan said. "Help me get this in the water."

Together, they safely carried the floatation device over the rocks, and into the water. Susan returned to the boat with a backpack strapped to her back. They loaded it into the floatation device, and started to sail into the ocean.

Susan dug into the bag and handed Pierce a bottle of water. They toasted each other, and drank to getting the fuck off of the island. After devouring several of the energy bars in the bag, they both couldn't help but fall asleep from extreme exhaustion.

* * *

When Pierce woke up, he heard a boat's motor. He wasn't sure how long he'd fallen asleep, but the sun was up high and blazing. Pierce told Susan to wake up, and that somebody was coming. The boat could've been a border patrol boat, or it could've been anybody. The red flashing lights didn't indicate who they represented.

Again, he was thrown into another dangerous situation. Once the boat reached their position, they were met by a group of individuals dressed in black military outfits. They clutched high-powered machine guns, and had the expressions of grizzled soldiers who'd seen many battles, and knew death up close and personal.

Pierce was in no condition to fight them.

Susan knew it too.

Whatever these people wanted with them, they would have no choice but to go along with it.

N.A.C.

Pierce didn't expect the sudden change of events. Pierce and Susan were enjoying cold beer and cold cut sandwiches. He was so grateful for food in his belly and alcohol in his veins. The people on the boat let them eat up their food before talking business.

The older military man introduced himself as Henry Garfield. Henry introduced his son, Duke, a shaven head G.I. Joe type, and a buzz haired woman named "Scoop". The last person on the boat handed Pierce another beer. This man easily had the biggest build of them all. He was a brick wall of muscular fortitude. He introduced himself as Anchor Stevens.

Henry did most of the talking. "You saved us a lot of time. Our mission was to infiltrate that island, take down Globo Corps's illegal dumpsite, and have our crews clean up the mess. The island was discovered only weeks ago, because Lee Branch has been monitored by our organization. We've tracked his movements to this island. When we realized there was much more on the island than chemicals, we had to reform our plan. Last night, we saw a war unfold. It's amazing anybody survived. You two have a lot going for you when it comes to fighting in the hot zone.

Anchor opened a beer, and raised his in cheers. "You dropped anchor on their asses."

"I'll be straight with you," Henry said, smiling at his outspoken partner. "We can't release you back into normal society. You know too much."

The hackles on Pierce's back went up like razor sharp quills.

He knew there was a catch coming.

"Whoa," Anchor said, reassuringly. "We're not the bad guys. Let the man finish."

Henry talked faster now. "I knew Angel, Pierce. I was familiar with her team of mercenaries. Hard Case, Shark, and Skeeter were all good people. We were close to asking them to join us in our mission until the plane accident. I'm so sorry, Pierce, for your loss."

Pierce had to know facts. Apologies wouldn't save anybody's life in this situation, and apologies surely wouldn't bring the dead back to life.

"Who are you? Who do you represent?"

"N.A.C.," Henry said with confidence. "The New American Coalition. We deal with unusual threats. Anything from naval threats, marine and aquatic threats, and now, environmental threats. A bigger problem lately has been mutation through the creation and dumping of illegal chemicals. Big companies like ENTECH and Global Corps are the key offenders. We're out to get them. Are you with us? I know Susan is from The Green Project. She'll be interested. You guys are perfect for the job. We need good people who can fight and think in tough situations. So how about it?"

Pierce felt the team's eyes burn into him.

"What happens if we say no?"

Henry sighed, "You'll be detained in a private prison indefinitely."

Anchor spoke. "That makes us sound like the bad guys. We don't want to jeopardize our cause. If anything leaks out, we lose our advantage against the enemy. The playing field is already in their favor, and we can't give up what little power we have."

He eyed Susan. Pierce could see the twinkle in her eye. Susan wanted in, and she didn't have to think about it to be sure. "I'm in. I'm the only living member of The Green Project. I want to keep fighting against those who keep wrecking this world. I'm sick of it. I'm tired of talking about it. I want to do something."

That left Pierce to consider his options. Join N.A.C., fight bad guys, or enjoy forced residency in a government compound.

He thought about Angel. Pierce hoped she'd be proud of him.

The choice was obvious.

"I'm in," Pierce said. "As long as there's a cold beer and a cheap sandwich at the end of every mission."

Anchor shook his hand. "Fuck yeah there is. If you find yourself balls deep in dinosaurs and cannibals and still come out of it in one piece, you're the kind of shit stomper we need on our team. Welcome to N.A.C."

"So what's the next mission?" Pierce asked.

Henry steered the boat back towards the United States. "The next mission? Well, that'll take some time to explain. *This one tops them all...*"

32079235R00081

Printed in Great Britain
by Amazon